HAR...

Presents

To all readers of Harlequin Presents

Thank you for your loyal
custom throughout 2006.

We look forward to bringing you the best
in intense, international and provocatively
passionate romance in 2007.

Happy holidays, and all good wishes
for the New Year!

Harlequin Presents®

GREEK TYCOONS

They're the men who have everything—
except brides...

Wealth, power, charm—
what else could a heart-stopplingly handsome
tycoon need? In the GREEK TYCOONS
miniseries you have already been introduced to
some gorgeous Greek multimillionaires who are
in need of wives.

Now it's the turn of favorite Harlequin Presents
author Cathy Williams, with her sensual
adventure *At the Greek Tycoon's Pleasure*.

This tycoon has met his match, and he's decided
he *has* to have her...*whatever* that takes!

Coming next month:

The Greek's Virgin
by Trish Morey
#2596

Cathy Williams

AT THE GREEK TYCOON'S PLEASURE

GREEK
TYCOONS

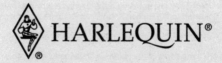

HARLEQUIN®

TORONTO • NEW YORK • LONDON
AMSTERDAM • PARIS • SYDNEY • HAMBURG
STOCKHOLM • ATHENS • TOKYO • MILAN • MADRID
PRAGUE • WARSAW • BUDAPEST • AUCKLAND

ISBN-13: 978-0-373-12592-0
ISBN-10: 0-373-12592-5

AT THE GREEK TYCOON'S PLEASURE

First North American Publication 2006.

Copyright © 2006 by Cathy Williams.

This edition published by arrangement with Harlequin Books S.A.

www.eHarlequin.com

Printed in U.S.A.

All about the author...
Cathy Williams

CATHY WILLIAMS was born in the West Indies and has been writing Harlequin romances for over fifteen years. She is a great believer in the power of perseverance as she had never written anything before and from the starting point of zero has now fulfilled her ambition to pursue this most enjoyable of careers. She would encourage any would-be writer to have faith and go for it!

She lives in the beautiful Warwickshire countryside with her husband and three children, Charlotte, Olivia and Emma. When not writing she is hard-pressed to find a moment's free time in between the millions of household chores, not to mention being a one-woman taxi service for her daughters' never-ending social lives.

She derives inspiration from the hot, lazy, tropical island of Trinidad (where she was born), from the peaceful countryside of middle England and, of course, from her many friends, who are a rich source of plots and are particularly garrulous when it comes to describing her heroes. It would seem from their complaints that tall, dark and charismatic men are too few and far between! Her hope is to continue writing romance fiction and providing those eternal tales of love for which, she feels, we all strive.

CHAPTER ONE

TIMOS HONOR looked at Theo over the rim of his wire-framed spectacles and stifled a sigh of compassion and sheer frustration. They both knew what he was going to say and the fact that Theo had had him flown over at great expense on his personal jet was not about to alter his recommendations.

'Spit it out, Timos.'

'There was no need to get me over here, Theo…'

'There was every need.' Theo's mouth thinned in hostile acceptance of what he knew he was going to hear. He was also well aware of the wisdom of Timos's words. He had already consulted the finest specialists that London could offer and been told the same thing. What had been the point of flying over Timos Honor, old family friend and top of his field in Greece? His story was going to be the same, but Theo had needed to hear it from one of his own, someone who might just be able to understand the torture he had been going through for the past eighteen months. Maybe he had needed to hear the stark reality with just a little bit of sympathetic packaging wrapped around it.

From the dubious sanctuary of his coldly minimalist penthouse apartment, Theo grimly regarded the thin, kindly man sitting in front of him.

'The bones in your foot have failed to heal properly and this second accident has only served to worsen the condition. What possessed you, man?'

'I wasn't skiing in the hope of finding the nearest obstacle into which I could collide, if that is what you mean.'

'You know it's not.' If Timos had had a full head of hair, he would have raked his fingers through it in exasperation. As it was, he made do with gently patting his balding head before linking his fingers on his lap. 'One skiing accident on a black run was bad enough, Theo, and we all understood the insanity that took you down that. Losing Elena just before you were due to be married... Well, it would be enough to send any sane man temporarily mad...but that was well over a year ago...'

'This last accident had nothing to do with Elena,' Theo said abruptly.

Of course it was a lie and he knew it. Theo was an accomplished skier. Recklessness had never been part of his agenda. But the past year and a half had seen him tackle the world with scant regard for himself. He had driven himself to exhaustion, working hours that no man was constructed to work, had embarked on deals that had made his cautious partners gasp and had only succeeded with them through good luck and his own staggering talent. Not once had he lost sleep over the fact that they might not have worked out. Great wealth, he supposed, brought freedom to be, frankly, adventurous. And, at the back of his mind, he was aware that something had to change. He couldn't keep living his life on the edge. He had to move on.

'Well, here is my diagnosis, for what it's worth, Theo. That foot of yours needs time to heal. You cannot continue putting it under strain. Nature has a cunning way of healing but this time you have pushed the boundaries too far and, if you do not give yourself some rest, the bones will never heal correctly and, at the very best, you will be left with a permanent limp that will put a stop to every type of sport. At the worst, you could eventually end up in a wheelchair, and let us not get into the very real possibility of premature arthritis. Tell me that that is what you want and I will heartily recommend that you take the next flight to Val d'Isère so that you can tackle another black run.'

They stared at each other in silence—Timos patiently waiting for his words to sink in, Theo bitterly aware that his behaviour had become perilously out of control. He was the first to look away with a scowl.

'So what do you suggest?' Theo finally asked, through gritted teeth.

'You need complete rest. You cannot keep covering the ground that you do. Your mother tells me that since your first accident you have barely stayed in one place long enough to have a hot meal.'

'Mama is prone to exaggeration.'

'As they all should be. But there is enough truth in her observation to warrant it in the first place.'

'I am a working man, Timos. Sitting around watching daytime television is not going to pay the bills.'

At that Timos laughed. 'You could retire tomorrow, Theo, and still have enough money to last several lifetimes over. And I am not suggesting that you go into hiding for the next two years. But you could slow down considerably. Work from home.' He glanced around the expensive apartment and shuddered at the thought of doing anything in it for any stretch of time. He, himself, lived with his adored wife in a small house on the outskirts of Athens that could not have been more different. This place reminded him of a crematorium—cold, marbled, immaculate but essentially lifeless.

'Three months would go a long way to restoring your mobility.'

'Three months!' Theo nearly burst out laughing.

'Delegate.' Timos stood up and collected his case from the side of his chair. 'A wise man knows when to.'

'And what the hell am I supposed to do for three months, Timos? Work from home and watch the walls?'

'Take up a hobby. Paint. Write poetry. Use the time to find yourself.'

The last thing Theo Andreou wanted to do was to find himself.

For the past two weeks—in fact, ever since Timos had delivered his parting shot—Theo had fought against the thought of holing up in his apartment with his foot up.

It had, he reflected now from the back seat of his chauffeur-driven Jaguar, been a losing battle because, hot on the heels of the doctor's uninvited pearls of wisdom, had come a barrage of phone calls from his mother in Greece. Roughly fifty per cent of them had involved pleas for him to come to Greece, where he could truly relax away from the pressures of London. When these had fallen on deaf ears, she had threatened to come over to England herself so that she could stay with him and make him take the time out that she claimed he needed. She had only relinquished her full frontal attack when he'd promised, swearing on the memory of his dead father, that he would leave London for a couple of months and kick about somewhere in the country. Somewhere peaceful where he would not be tempted to darken the doors of his exquisite office at the drop of a hat.

He tore his gaze away from the sullen October skies

outside and did his best to focus on the colour brochure lying on his lap. He actually hadn't even seen the cottage his car was speeding towards. The deal had been done by his personal assistant, who had located the required peaceful spot and determined the necessary small but delightful cottage whose task was to provide him with rest, recuperation and not too much by way of hard work.

The fact that the place was in Cornwall was designed to deter him from any spontaneous swoops into the office.

Gloria had personally seen the place, checked out the shops nearby, made sure that it wasn't too far removed from civilisation and arranged for a housekeeper to come in every other day to keep it in order. Someone else would cook for him. His role would be to appreciate the scenery, do a little work now and again and have lots of early nights.

Theo was dreading the whole thing.

Thank God for the invention of the laptop computer and mobile phones.

'Slow down when you drive through the village,' he said to his chauffeur, dumping the brochure on top of his case and staring out of the window. 'I want to see exactly what I'm supposed to be enjoying for the next two months.'

And there it was, suddenly in front of him, the town clinging to the sides of a hill, an engaging mixture of old and not so old buildings. Just out of sight, he knew the River Dart flowed from the wilds of Dartmoor before entering the sea just here. It was picturesque and, more importantly, not nearly so small and backward as he had imagined. Theo gave silent thanks to Gloria, who obviously knew him well enough to realise that too much nature would not be a blessing in disguise. From what he could make out, there were restaurants, cafés, some shops, at least the comfortable trappings of civilisation.

The car swerved away from the town, heading south, just as his eyes focused on the figure of a girl trying to shut the door of a small office that looked more like a house than a place of work. She was struggling with it and, for a few wild, disconcerting seconds, Theo felt his heart race. From behind, whoever she was reminded him swiftly and poignantly of Elena. Same slight frame and fair hair falling straight to her shoulders. Then he blinked and was angrily aware that his mind had drifted again.

With formidable control Theo slammed shut the door on the painful memories that were always trying to fight their way out and concentrated on the picturesque drive towards the cottage.

There had been no exaggeration on the part of the estate agents. The cottage, when it finally came into view, was every bit as charming as it appeared to be in its picture. At nearly four-thirty in the afternoon, the already fading light picked up the yellow tint of the walls and turned them into burnished gold. The garden, which was not small, was lovingly pruned and trimmed back and the small path that led up to the house was exactly like something out of a child's story book.

His mother, he had no doubt, would have heartily approved. She had always disliked his penchant for the ultra-modern.

'You can drive the car to the station when you're done here, Jimmy.' He let himself out of the car and, with the aid of a stick, something he frankly found ridiculous and largely un-necessary, he began walking towards the front door, key in hand. 'Just bring the bags in. No need for you to stay.'

'I should make sure that everything is okay…'

Theo spared him a frowning backward glance. Since when had the world started feeling sorry for him?

'I think I can handle it from here. Apparently the housekeeper's coming round in about an hour to check and make sure everything's in place.' He tried to temper the harshness of his voice with a smile. 'No point having two people falling over themselves in a small house checking the locks on the doors. If you leave the car at the station I can find a way of getting to it if I need it.'

'Of course, sir.'

As soon as the man had gone, Theo sank on to the sofa and stared around him.

Without the comforting sounds of distant cars and sirens outside, the silence around him seemed oppressive and unfamiliar. He spent a few well used minutes cursing his decision to listen to the combined exhortations of Timos and his mother and wondering what in hell he was going to do with any time not spent in front of his computer or on the phone. Such as now. He even missed the social life in London, which had always seemed to be forcing itself down his throat when he least needed it. But it had been contact.

With a dark scowl, he tramped his way upstairs and was in the process of doing something he had seldom done in his life before, namely unpacking his own bags, when he heard the trill of the doorbell.

On the other side of the door, Sophie Scott wrapped her jacket more tightly around her. Her scowl matched Theo's.

This was the first time the cottage was being rented since she had moved out two months previously and she liked it as little as she had expected. She had tried to make the place as impersonal as possible, but she knew that there were reminders of her past happy life spent there with her father everywhere. From the books she hadn't been able to transfer to her own much smaller rented accommodation in the flat above the office, to the linen, which was freshly laundered but still a legacy of the past, to the flowers in the garden, each one of which seemed capable of propelling her down memory lane.

She heard the heavy shuffle of approaching footsteps and her whole body stiffened in response.

The smile she tried hard to pin on her face threatened to harden into a grimace and she reminded herself what the lawyer had told her. That she needed the money. Ideally she should sell the house, but if not she would simply have to rent it. It could fetch a great deal of money, particularly in the summer months. Cornwall was a very desirable tourist destination and getting more so. Blah, blah, blah.

The door was pulled open and, for a few heart-stopping seconds, Sophie's mind went completely blank as she took in the man standing in front of her.

He was very tall—over six foot—and was not the middle-aged oily Greek man she had conjured up in her imagination. Nothing oily about him at all. In fact, he was handcrafted perfection. His hair was raven-black and swept away from his face and his eyes were the green of perfect Cornish seas, but it was the angles of his face that struck her most because they gave his flawless features a harsh, powerful beauty.

He was wearing casual clothes, a faded shirt rolled to the elbows and a pair of weathered jeans that moulded his long legs. She managed to keep her gawping eyes under control, but she was well aware that his body was every bit as impressive as his face.

'You must be the housekeeper.'

Sophie opened her mouth to explain the situation in no uncertain terms and shut it. He had stood aside to let her enter and she brushed past him, suspiciously looking around, checking to see if anything had been broken, which was unlikely considering he had only been in the place for a matter of a couple of hours. Still.

She was skin-tinglingly aware of his eyes on her—green, green shuttered eyes, and it made her feel clumsy and awkward.

'When did you arrive?'

'About an hour ago. No time to make any mess yet, but feel free to inspect the premises.' Theo now recognised her. The fair hair, the colour of vanilla ice cream, the slender frame. Along with recognition came a certain amount of resentment that he could have confused her with Elena, even if it had only been for a few passing seconds. Up close, this woman was nothing like his fiancée. Her eyes were brown, not cornflower-blue, and her skin still carried the golden stain of summer. Elena, so wildly different from every Greek girl he had ever known, had been a fair-haired beauty, courtesy of her Scandinavian mother. She had not been able to cope well with the sun, always making sure that she wore hats, large straw things that emphasised her fragility. This woman was more robust-looking.

As was the direct expression on her face.

'I'm not here to inspect the premises,' Sophie told him bluntly. 'I'm here to make sure that you're satisfied with the food I've bought for you and to find out whether you know where everything is and how everything works. And I'm not the housekeeper. The housekeeper is a girl called Annie and she'll be with you the day after tomorrow. Catherine is the lady you employed to cook your food and that's all she'll do. Cook and do the dishes. You'll be expected to take care of the rest.'

'If you're not the housekeeper and you're not the cook, then would you mind telling me exactly who you are?' Theo maintained a semblance of politeness with difficulty. Bad enough to find himself in the middle of nowhere without having to deal with unexplained hostility from a woman who hadn't yet seen fit to introduce herself. 'Because I don't think I got your name. And for the astronomical sum of money I'm forking out for this place, I expect a certain amount of civility.'

Sophie felt colour crawl into her cheeks.

'I apologise if I seemed a bit…a bit…abrupt…' she said. Her mouth tried a smile, which wasn't replicated in her eyes. Just the man's presence in her house—*her* house—made her bristle with resentment. 'I should have introduced myself at the start.' She held out her hand. 'My name's Sophie Scott and I own this cottage, actually.'

'Then you might want to start thinking about being polite to the person paying the rent.' Theo ignored the outstretched hand. He couldn't imagine how he could ever have confused her with his beloved Elena. He couldn't imagine Elena ever being rude to a stranger, but then again English women could be odd. Having lived in London for well over eight years, he still found their forwardness amusing and distasteful at the same time. This one seemed to be of the same mould as all the rest.

He was aware of her following him, something he found highly irritating when all he wanted to do was settle down in front of his computer with a glass of wine and check his email.

He headed towards the kitchen, pulled open the fridge and stared at the contents. 'There's no wine in here.'

'No, *Mr Andreou*, I thought you might want to choose your alcohol yourself. If you were that keen on drinking as soon as you arrived, you should have informed us and we could have sorted something out for you.'

Theo narrowed his eyes on her, shut the door of the fridge

and sat at the pine kitchen table. Her face was perfectly still and courteous but was there some insolent implication in her words that pointed to him being a drunk?

For the first time in as long as he could recall, the demonic thoughts that plagued him night and day disappeared under his sheer annoyance at the creature standing unapologetically in front of him.

'Well, maybe you would like to sort something out for me now. Wine. White. Preferably a Chablis. You can tack the cost of it on to my bill at the end of the month and throw in extra for inconvenience caused.'

'Of course, Mr Andreou, although I really need to be getting back home now. Would it be possible for you to wait for your wine until tomorrow? I could send Annie along with a selection of whites for you.'

'Possible, but not desirable. I've had a long and tiring journey here and a glass of chilled wine is really what I'd like.'

He had no idea why he was pushing the point. He had done a certain number of reckless things since Elena's accident but drowning his sorrows in drink hadn't been one of them. In fact, he had avoided alcohol for the most part. Looking at Sophie's ramrod figure, however, he could only think that her simmering anger at his high-handed attitude made a pleasant change from the soft shuffle of people tiptoeing around him just in case they said the wrong thing.

'Right. Would there be anything else?'

'Just the wine.'

Sophie nodded and headed out of the door. Theo was frankly surprised that she didn't slam it shut behind her, but then again, if the house belonged to her she would have no choice but to pander to her tenant. A tenant who was paying top whack even though the high season was emphatically over.

It was all of fifteen minutes before Sophie returned, the cool night air having done very little to improve her frame of mind.

Yes, he might be a writer, and writers were notoriously moody and temperamental, but that was no excuse to be downright rude. Maybe, she fumed, clutching the bag containing two bottles of wine, because clearly he bordered on alcoholic if he couldn't keep away from the stuff for a few hours, he thought that his looks gave him some kind of imperious right to do away with the need to be considerate.

She toyed with the seductive scenario of telling him that he could find somewhere else to stay, that she would rather have no tenant than a tenant like him.

Common sense plastered a polite smile back on to her face as the door was opened and she felt as taken aback by his physical appearance as she had the first time round.

'The wine.' She held out the carrier bag and kept well behind the threshold.

'Join me.'

'I beg your pardon?'

'For a drink. By way of apology for my arrogant behaviour.' Theo directed a smile at her that made her blink in sudden confusion.

It was a smile he had not used for a long time. For years, an ever changing assortment of beautiful women had been the object of his massive charm. Then he had met Elena, quite accidentally at his mother's house on one of his quick stop overs. The stop over had lasted ten days longer than he had originally planned and, at the end of it, he had left an engaged man, smitten with the young golden-haired girl who had agreed to be his wife. Five months later Elena had been killed and with her his dreams of marriage and family. Since then, and despite the women who still flocked around him, Theo had remained steadfastly and bitterly celibate. The easy charm that had seen him fêted as the most eligible bachelor in London, the biggest catch in the sea, had been locked away behind a forbidding coldness that could deter even the most persistent.

He realised that he must be feeling ridiculously uneasy with his surroundings to have encouraged the woman to stay. Especially when she was now staring at him like a wild animal caught in a trap with no visible means of escape.

'I'm not sure that would be entirely appropriate, Mr Andreou…'

'Why not?' He headed towards the kitchen, eschewing the walking stick but taking it slowly. Despite what the doctors had said, putting pressure on the foot had seemed to encourage a healthy immunity to the pain and discomfort. A day spent sitting in a car had now made him realise how tender it still was and he scowled at the limitations of a body that had never in his life let him down before.

Sophie closed the door quietly behind her and counted to ten. She reminded herself that she had to be polite. As the odious man had pointed out, he was paying her bills.

'Aren't you tired?' She followed him into the kitchen and avoided his question by going down a different route. Watching from the kitchen door, he didn't *look* tired. In fact, he didn't strike her as the sort of man who *ever* succumbed to something as routine as exhaustion, but he wasn't walking properly. 'I know that trip down from London can be a killer, especially when there's traffic around. Although I guess you travelled down by train. I didn't notice any car parked outside.'

'Big house for one person, or were you living here with someone else?'

Sophie drew in a deep breath and kept trying to smile. 'Big

house for a single man to rent, or are you intending to bring down someone else to keep you company?'

Theo turned and looked at her, one hand on the bottle, the other slowly drawing out the cork. His impression of her was deteriorating by the second. Added to the unacceptable insolence, he could sense simmering just beneath the surface a stubbornness that was only thinly disguised by the stiff smile on her face.

'I mean…' Sophie continued hastily, stepping into the kitchen and sitting down at the table, the old, worn pine table that had seen a thousand meals and school books and, later on, art work and designs '…Cornwall is very popular with families… Do you have a family, Mr Andreou?'

Theo yanked out the cork and poured two glasses of wine.

'There is no need to call me Mr Andreou. The name is Theo.' He placed a glass in front of her and was relieved to sit down and give his foot a rest.

'And will you be bringing your family down at some point, Mr And…Theo? Or do you prefer to have solitude for your writing?' Sophie sipped the wine and decided that she had made a good choice. She didn't know too much about it, but obviously going for the most expensive bottle in the off licence had been a good idea.

'I beg your pardon?' About to deliver a short, sharp sermon on which subject she would do well to avoid, Theo was caught on the back foot by her remark. Did the woman seriously imagine that any single man renting a cottage by the sea was automatically a writer?

'I asked whether you planned on bringing…'

'I have no family, Miss Scott.'

'Right.'

'You were asking about…my writing…?'

'Yes. I just wondered whether you rented the cottage because you needed to be on your own to write.' She took another gulp of the wine. Meeting the man's gaze was next to impossible. Those fabulous eyes were doing weird things to her.

'And you think I am a writer because…?'

'Because Johnny told me. I'm sorry. I realise that it's none of my business. Actually, I should be on my way.' She half stood up.

'Sit back down!'

Sophie literally jumped at the command and glared at him. 'Shouldn't writers be a bit more *sensitive*?' she snapped. Politeness flew out of the window as did the last residue of her patience. 'Shouting at people is no way to behave, Mr Andreou! And, I tell you this right now—if you intend to act in that manner, then I shall have no option but to withdraw the services of Catherine and Annie. They're both sweet-tempered girls and I won't have you yelling at them!'

It was one of those extremely rare moments in Theo's life when he was literally lost for words.

He was a man who had become accustomed to saying exactly what he wanted and to having his orders followed. Indeed, there was rarely any need for him to even raise his voice. He spoke and others obeyed. It was as simple as that.

He looked at her rising colour and knew that the best thing he could do would be to tell her to go. She was too abrasive, too outspoken, and a personality clash was the last thing he either needed or felt inclined to deal with.

'You haven't finished your wine, Miss Scott,' he countered mildly. 'Why don't you finish it and tell me who this Johnny character is? I don't approve of having my personal life discussed behind my back. Gossip is something I have little time for.'

Sophie clasped the edge of the table and breathed deeply. How many times could one person count to ten before it lost its value as a calming mechanism? How *dared* he imply that she was a *gossip?*

She sat back down as calmly as she could manage. 'I don't gossip, Mr Andreou.'

'Theo. I told you.'

Sophie ignored the interruption. 'John Taylor is the man at the estate agency who arranged this letting. Apparently the lady working on your behalf informed him that you would be here to do a bit of writing. He thought it useful to let me know because he knew that I was reluctant... Well, let's just say that it was important for me to know that you weren't going to be the sort of tenant to wreck the house. There have been a few incidents here over the years where houses have been let to people in the movie industry and damage has been caused by wild parties and the like. So we weren't *gossiping* about you. It was an exchange of factual information.'

Theo smiled at the thought of Gloria protecting his identity. But writer? He wondered what sort of books he would be interested in writing.

'What sort of books do you write?'

'Ah. Thrillers, as a matter of fact.'

Sophie felt curiosity reluctantly creep under her skin. 'What sort of thrillers? You must write under a pseudonym...'

'Perhaps *thrillers* isn't quite the right description for my...ah...books...' Theo said. As conversations went, it was bizarre but strangely liberating not to be typecast as the formidable and extremely powerful businessman deserving of the greatest respect, if not downright fear. 'More factual accounts of people who have been in life-threatening situations. Right now I am working on something to do with black runs.'

Sophie could make sense of that. The man exuded an air of danger. It seemed fitting that he would write about lives lived on the edge.

'Must be very exciting for you—making a living doing what you love—writing about the things that interest you. Much more stimulating than some boring office job somewhere in the city!' She thought of the boring office job which she had been compelled to take. Her father might have been interested in all manner of medical things but his passion for invention had turned out to be more than an amusing hobby to keep his brain ticking over. He had, it turned out in the messy wake of his death, poured money into his obsession with *creating* any manner of things, helped struggling scientists and inventors and literally travelled the breadth and width of the country over the years, going to various science shows and turning small overnight trips into week-long stops. And spending money with the absent-minded innocence of someone quite clueless when it came to all things financial. Leaving her here now, doing her best to clear things up.

She dragged herself away from the depressing thoughts and looked at Theo from under her lashes.

'Would I have read any of your books? I mean, what name do you write under? How far have you got on the one you're working on?'

'I really would rather not discuss my writing.' Theo poured himself another glass of wine and relaxed back in the chair. 'Tell me about the village. I shall probably have to venture into it at some point.'

Putting her in her place. That was the impression that Sophie got. In not so many words, he was telling her to mind her own business and, for the life of her, she couldn't figure out why he would be so secretive about what he did for a living. Shouldn't he be promoting his books? After all, she *was* a member of the public and it *was* a buying public who kept him in this lifestyle.

And a very good lifestyle, considering the amount he was paying for the use of her cottage, not to mention the housekeeper and the cook. She glanced at him, to find that he was looking at her with a cool shuttered expression, almost as though he was waiting for her to digest the conversational boundaries he was laying down.

Nothing personal, in fact. And his remark about gossiping had been a warning that she should steer clear of talking about him behind his back. Maybe he thought that, simple peasant lass that she was, the only thing that preoccupied her would be shooting her mouth off about the mysterious handsome stranger in the cottage.

She returned his cool expression with one of her own and began telling him about the basic shops in the village and where he could go if he wanted to explore further afield. As she spoke, she began getting to her feet and tightening her jacket around her, noticing that he was not bothering to stand up. In fact, he dragged over a chair and propped his feet up on it. Sophie resisted the urge to tell him to remove them.

'And do you live in this exciting little village?'

'Yes, as a matter of fact, I do.'

'And how do you amuse yourself in the evenings?' He fleetingly wondered whether she had a boyfriend or not and decided that she probably didn't. What man could ever be attracted to a woman with such a sharp tongue? Elena, he thought painfully, had been angelically soft spoken. He snapped out of his thoughts to hear the tail-end of a sentence and registered that whatever had been said had been yet another example of unladylike sarcasm. He could tell from

the badly concealed aggression of her stance. Hand on hip.
Fist curled tightly around the strap of her bag.

'What did you say?'

'You asked me how I amused myself in this *exciting little
village*.' She could tell that his thoughts had been miles away,
probably on a ski slope with some cutting edge daredevil, the
likes of whom would never darken her *exciting little village*.
The man who had *invaded* her cottage now saw fit to sneer
at the lifestyle it represented! 'Mostly we just sit around in
the local, wearing our cloth caps, with twigs in our mouths,
knocking back the ale.'

'I think it's time for you to leave now,' Theo told her coldly.
'Thank you for the wine and don't forget to put it on my bill.'

Sophie could have kicked herself. She knew she should,
but she just couldn't bring herself to issue another apology.
For starters, he would recognise it for the meaningless words
that they were because she didn't feel very apologetic. The
man was arrogant and unbearable. Fat, short, oily and middle-aged would have been infinitely preferable. Instead, she
nodded and mouthed some nonsense about feeling free to call
her any time if he had any complaints whatsoever. Ironic
when his complaints would probably be about her and her
attitude.

'I hope you enjoy your stay,' she managed to get out, along
with a forced smile.

Torn between the need to dither and at least put on a show
of being a thoughtful landlady and the desire to walk out as
fast as her legs could take her, Sophie remained where she was
until Theo walked to the fridge and, with his back to her, left
her in no doubt that she could go. She did. Fuming and red-
faced and consoling herself with the thought that his fat cheque
would be worth the headache of knowing he was in her space.

Chilled by the night air, she finally managed to gather her scattered thoughts and reach a decision—she would leave him to his own devices, get Annie and Catherine to report back to her about the state of the house and count the weeks till he disappeared back up to London.

CHAPTER TWO

ARE you sure you are following the doctor's orders and resting? Does your foot feel any better? Yes, we're managing just fine here. Of course I'll sort out those conference calls, but are you quite sure you shouldn't just be resting?

At the end of four interminably long days and even longer nights, Theo could feel his head clanging with the repeated urges from the entire world, it seemed, that he relax. He had been assured by Gloria so many times that it was business as usual that he had been forced to cut her short on a couple of occasions rather than sit through the inevitable ramblings about his need to take it easy.

Taking it easy had never been one of Theo's greatest talents and he was finding it exceptionally difficult to adhere to now.

It was mid-afternoon. The house had been cleaned so thoroughly that any lingering bacteria would have had a struggle to stage a comeback. He had eaten the pasta which the cook had prepared and his conference call had ended over an hour ago.

Outside, a cold breeze was threatening to turn into a gale. Even through the small window panes, he could appreciate the wildness of the scenery. It occurred to him that, apart from a couple of visits to the garden, he hadn't been outside the house for days. Not since that aggravating woman had left, in fact.

For once, the image of a woman other than Elena crossed his mind. The slight frame that should have heralded a demure personality but didn't. The stubborn mouth which looked as though it had been having a hard time trying not to rebel against the smile she had pasted on. The flashing brown eyes, narrowed to suspicious slits and ready to glare.

He felt a reluctant smile curve his mouth.

It disappeared as swiftly as it had surfaced. Uttering an oath under his breath, Theo slammed shut his computer, shoved his cellphone into his pocket and headed out of the cottage with his thick jacket slung over his shoulders.

It was as cold outside as it had looked. And as scenic. Having been to places in the world most people had only ever dreamed of, Theo wondered how it was that he seemed to be seeing what was around him for the first time. The downside of zero distractions, he assumed, considering the majority of his visits to exotic places had taken place under the mantle of work.

Out the cottage, the small lane towards the village was lined with a selection of shrubbery, stripped at this time of year of its greenery and jostling for space. And the clean, salty smell of the air was pungent enough to make him gasp.

The routine of exercise he had been sticking to made use of the stick less necessary but he had brought it along with him anyway. Every so often, he swiped some of the shrubbery at the side and scowled impatiently at the sneaky feeling of boyishness it gave him.

The first thing he glimpsed as he turned the corner was her office.

There it was, fronted by lovingly cared for plants on the

outside and resembling not so much an office as somewhere casual in which to relax.

He thought it typical. Her behaviour towards him had not marked her out as a professional woman with her finger on the pulse. Any competent career woman would know that to expose her feelings was tantamount to waving the white flag.

Feet that should have been walking to the café next to the office paused and, before he knew it, he was rapping his stick on the office door, pushing it open into a scene of seeming chaos. In the middle of this chaos, Sophie stood with one hand raked through her fair hair in frustration, peering and frowning at a piece of paper in her hand. Around her, three people appeared to be doing things, though what Theo couldn't begin to fathom. Two women and a fair-haired man, who looked at him and smiled with good-natured curiosity.

He was already regretting the insane impulse that had prompted his appearance.

He must, he thought sourly, be in need of company even though he had never considered himself the sort of man who craved the presence of other people, especially in the last few months when memories had been the only things to share the space in his head.

'Soph, you have a visitor.'

From across the room, Sophie glanced up, plucked out of her little world of trying to figure out what the heck this latest scribbled piece of paper was supposed to signify. Another bill? Of sorts? Something that had been returned for a credit that would not be chanced upon any time soon?

It was only when her eyes tangled with Theo's that she realised how much she had been thinking about him—off and on for four days—and even though she felt nettled every single time he had crossed her mind, she still hadn't been able to erase the image from her head.

Her skin tingled in sudden awareness of his eyes on her and the impossibly sexy slant of his body as he lounged indolently against the doorframe, taking in the scene in front of him.

'Oh. It's you.' She looked around and introduced him indifferently to Moira, Claire and, of course, Robert. 'This is Mr Andreou, the man from the cottage. How can I help you?' Her feet suddenly felt like lead and she translated the heat racing through her body as an angry reaction to the fact that, not content with living in her cottage, he was now invading the privacy of her working space.

She reluctantly walked towards him, aware that all eyes were on her.

'I was just out for a walk and I thought I'd drop in.'

'How did you know where I worked?'

'Saw you here when I arrived, as a matter of fact. You were locking up behind you.'

'There was no need for you to come here, Mr Andreou...'

'When do you intend to start calling me *Theo*?' he asked, suddenly irritated.

'*Theo*. I wrote down my telephone number and left it by the phone book on the table in the hall. I believe I told you that.'

'So this is where you work...' He pushed himself away from the doorframe and was confronted by Robert, who offered his hand by way of a more formal introduction.

'The name's Robert Bell. Your face looks familiar. Have I met you somewhere before?'

'No,' Theo said flatly, ignoring the outstretched hand and moving towards one of the desks on which he perched, while Sophie looked on, mouth agape at the sheer nerve of the man.

'You probably recognise him from the cover of a book somewhere. Theo's a writer.'

'In the presence of fame,' Robert remarked, grinning. 'Aren't you lucky, Soph? You can take his picture and build up a wall of fame over the years! Do wonders for the rental income, you know.' He moved to sling one arm over Sophie's shoulder and she eased herself away and towards Theo, now idly rifling through the reams of disorganised paperwork on her desk.

'You never said what you wanted. Is everything all right with the cottage? Are Catherine and Annie working out okay?' She snatched the papers from him and dumped them back on the desk.

He had, she noticed abstractedly, great hands. Strong, with long fingers and sufficient dark hair curling at the strap of his watch to make her wonder whether he had hair on his chest or not. She caught herself midway through the treacherous uninvited thought and frowned at him.

'Fine. The house is beyond clean and the food is beyond good.'

'Then why are you here?' Sophie asked bluntly. 'I have an awful lot of work to get through and I really can't spare the time for chit-chat.'

Theo looked around him. 'You do seem to be a bit…overwhelmed here…'

'Not *overwhelmed*, just…'

'Trying to impose order on chaos…' Robert approached them and clicked his tongue in good-natured reprimand at Sophie. 'Sophie has inherited all this from her father and…'

'Do you mind, Robert? I'm sure Mr…Theo…isn't interested in all of that!' She tempered the sharpness of her reply with an apologetic smile and gave his arm a brief warm squeeze. All said and done, Robert had been her rock in recent

months, sacrificing quite a bit of his free time to help her out, taking her out for the odd pizza when she had been feeling particularly down, always looking on the bright side of things. Yes, they went back a few years, but there was no way that she was going to take him for granted!

'What sort of job was your father in?' Theo asked, curious now that she had made a point of trying to steer him away from her boundaries. 'Was he a doctor?'

'Why do you say that?'

'Because the papers seem to indicate a medical bent.'

Sophie's mouth dropped open and she shut it quickly. She didn't care what he thought of her, but the gaping goldfish impression wasn't an attractive one.

'Dad trained as a pharmacist, if you must know, and after he retired he dabbled here in one or two things…' Talking about him still upset her and she turned away and walked towards another part of the office where yet more boxes awaited inspection. 'Now, I really must ask you to leave. I have heaps to do.' She busied herself with the little bundle of files on the desk.

'Take a break. Join me for a cup of coffee at the café next door.' Theo was mildly surprised that he had offered the invitation and he wasn't at all surprised when she turned him down. 'There are, actually, one or two things I need to discuss with you about the cottage.'

'I thought you said everything was fine.' Sophie looked at him anxiously. From the laborious process of going through her father's belongings, one thing was becoming clearer and clearer by the day. His assets were heavily compromised. Invoices for supplies of substances she could barely pronounce, never mind recognise, littered the office. There were people waiting by the door for payment. Most weren't as yet baying, because her father had been a lovable man and had obviously surrounded himself with very loyal and supportive people, even the ones waiting to have their bills met, but her father was no longer around and it wouldn't be long before the patient waiting turned ugly. No one, owed money, remained jolly indefinitely.

The cottage was his greatest asset and she had to make a go of renting it because she just couldn't bring herself to sell it.

If Theo wasn't happy then her bank manager wasn't going to be happy either.

'What kind of things?' she asked with a worried frown.

'We could discuss this next door…' He watched as she glanced hesitantly around the office and ran her fingers through her hair. She looked frazzled. Her blonde hair was pulled back into a ponytail that had probably commenced the day in a far neater condition than it was now. And Robert, he noticed, was eager for the role of protector, rushing to her side and patting her gently on the back, leaning over to whisper something in her ear. The other two women, both middle-aged, glanced at each other covertly and buried themselves in whatever they had been doing before he had interrupted their afternoon.

The dynamics of a provincial office. If *office* wasn't a laughable overstatement, because nothing here resembled Theo's offices—a huge smoked glass building, with each of its eight floors devoted to the efficient running of an empire that had tentacles stretching from his inherited shipping business to a thousand other concerns, all thriving, all diverse. And, at the top of the impressive building, a monument to modern architecture, sat Theo's domain, a suite of partitioned offices where members of his close staff worked in silent productivity.

He dragged his attention back to Sophie, who was trying hard now to produce a crisp businesslike manner which was not in keeping with the ruffled hair, the flushed cheeks and the casual attire of faded jeans and an oversized rugby shirt.

'I guess I could spare a few minutes,' she conceded. He must think her blind not to have noticed the scathing look he gave her premises. He might be a hot shot writer, but she doubted he would have known where to start if he had been in her shoes. She grabbed her bag which, as usual, seemed to be stuffed with too many things and nodded at him. 'I'll only be a short while,' she said to the others, smiling when Moira told her to take her time, that they were fine to carry on sifting through the paperwork without her for a bit.

'I would appreciate it if you could phone me with queries in the future,' was the first thing she said as they left the office. 'I realise that I'm responsible for what goes on in the cottage but, unless it's an absolute emergency, I would rather you waited until after working hours.' Next to him, she felt ridiculously small yet she was an average five foot six. He just seemed very tall and very big. Oppressive, in fact, she thought. And how did he manage to look so *expensive* when he was really only wearing some cords and a cream jumper with a very ordinary suede jacket? She glanced across at him, cross with herself for letting him get to her. Again.

He pushed open the door to the café without answering and Sophie slipped past him, brushing against the suede jacket and feeling her body stiffen in sudden self-consciousness.

'So what seems to be the problem? You said that Catherine and Annie were doing their jobs…'

'To perfection…'

'Then what?'

At three-thirty on a cold autumn afternoon, Theo was amused to see that the café was practically full. Old biddies were chatting over plates of scones and pots of tea. Where the hell did they find the time? At three-thirty in the afternoon, in London, or New York or Paris or Tokyo, he would have been chairing a high-powered meeting or pacing his office, with his PA there, rattling off a million and one things that needed to be done sooner than yesterday and preferably sooner than the day before. He would have kept going, sometimes until late into the night when exhaustion would finally kick in and sleep would be the only option. An option he would have delayed forever because with sleep came the memories.

What was it with the time down here? It seemed to be like elastic, stretching interminably in a twenty-four hour period. Even with his calls, his emails, his extensive reports, he still seemed to have time on his hands at the end of the day.

These people here seemed to have nothing better to do than while away the time over tea and cakes.

He found that he himself was ordering a pot of tea, when the waitress came across.

'So?' Sophie prompted. Those unsettling green eyes rested on her face and she flushed.

'It's the heating,' Theo found himself improvising. Now that he was up close and watching her squarely in the face, he could see that her huge brown eyes were fringed with thick, very dark lashes which made a startling contrast to the blonde hair. 'I'm afraid you'll have to show me the workings.' Theo had never asked anyone to help him with anything for as long as he could remember and certainly never something as fundamentally straightforward as the heating system of a house. If his mother could hear him now, she would roar with laughter, he thought uncomfortably. 'Not that I can't figure it out on my own…' sheer Greek pride forced him to qualify.

Sophie looked at him warily, then she smiled. So he *did*

have chinks in that armour! Even though he came across as the sort of man who could climb Mount Everest during his lunch break!

That genuine hesitant smile was disconcerting enough to make Theo frown, and Sophie, seeing the frown, misinterpreted it as embarrassment at being caught out unable to succeed at doing something.

'I know,' she said with pseudo-concern, 'it's terrible for a man having to admit that he actually can't do something, isn't it?' She thought back to the many DIY jobs her father had attempted doing, only to end up calling in the experts. He had been clever at science and enthralled at what mankind was capable of inventing, but show him a flat pack and he had inevitably been stuck. 'Still, you're a writer so I suppose you have an excuse.'

'And why is that?'

'Because writers aren't really supposed to know how to do practical stuff, like working out the heating or fixing a washer or…replacing a light bulb.'

Theo was outraged at her generalised assumption that he was a woolly-headed idiot but condemned to accept it with grudging good humour. He wondered why he had conjured up such a ridiculous story. Frankly, he wondered why he had bothered. People had already called to find out whether he needed company, including one acquaintance, Yvonne, who had mistakenly translated his previously polite responses as active encouragement. So why the hell was he seeking out the company of a woman who, aside from everything else, did not have a respectful bone in her body?

'Is that right?' he drawled, sitting back and sipping some of the tea and watching as she tucked into the obligatory scone with jam and cream.

'Yes. Although maybe you're different as you don't write fiction.'

Theo watched her lick a drop of cream from her finger. His so-called profession was something he certainly did not wish to linger upon.

'Okay, I'll pop in after work and have a look. There shouldn't be a problem, really. One thing we've always made sure to look after has been the heating system in the house. It gets too cold here to take any chances.'

'You being…you and your father…'

Sophie stilled. She wiped her fingers on the napkin and looked across to the waitress for the bill.

'That's right,' she said. 'So, if anything, the timer switch needs adjusting. I should have thought that you would want the heating on more than normal because you're probably indoors all day working.' The bill came and she protested vigorously when Theo insisted on paying.

'How did he die?'

He wasn't overstepping the mark—Sophie knew that. He was being polite, maybe even sympathetic, but she still resented the question. It was none of his business. Asking her personal questions was out of line. He was a tenant, not a friend, and not even a particularly nice tenant.

'I assume it's not a secret,' Theo said dryly, 'but if you'd rather change the subject, then that's fine.'

'He had a heart attack. It was quite sudden. He wasn't old and he was very fit and healthy.'

The memory of Elena's death came back to him with such ferocity that he drew in his breath. A different start to her day, a different road travelled, maybe not stopping to take his call, and her life would not have shattered into a thousand pieces.

'So you have been left to sort out his affairs,' he said

abruptly and Sophie, relieved to escape the sadness of the topic, grasped the diversion gratefully and nodded.

'It's a bit of a mess, to be honest. I guess I'll have to get some financial person in at some point to help, but right now I'm doing the best I can.' She looked at her watch and stood up. 'Will you be staying on here for another pot of tea?' she asked politely. 'Because I've got to go now. It's a bit cold and breezy, but the shops will be open for another hour or so and you could explore.'

'I might,' Theo said dismissively, having no intention of doing any such thing. 'And I'll see you…at what time…?'

'Oh, about six, once I've locked up.'

It was a Friday night. She was a young girl. Yes, the area might not be hopping with wild night excitement, but had she nowhere to go?

Curiosity, like some alien virus, entered his bloodstream and he stood up, waiting for her to leave before heading back to the cottage. Where he cleverly adjusted a couple of switches so that his ridiculous story could be corroborated.

For once, the panacea of work took a back seat. Gloria phoned, updating him on various deals he had on the go, filling him in on the snippets of gossip, in which he was not the slightest interested. As she spoke, Theo thought about Sophie, then slammed shut the door on the thoughts the second he became aware of them.

At six he heard the buzz of the doorbell and there she was when he pulled open the door. No longer in her jeans and rugby shirt, but combat trousers and a cream sweater over which she wore a longish olive-green jacket that engulfed her. The rumpled hair was now brushed and tied back into two little plaits that made her look about fifteen.

'On time,' he said, stepping aside and watching as she

walked into the hall and deposited her coat on the banister
with the familiarity of someone who had probably spent a
lifetime doing it.

'I live just above the office. It takes me all of ten minutes
to get here.' Sophie looked around, expecting and finding the
house in impeccable condition. Annie and Catherine would
have told her if he had been a slob. He might be arrogant,
obnoxious and full of himself but at least he was relatively
tidy. No sign of anything, not even the reams of paper she
would have expected to be piling up somewhere. He
probably just wrote directly on to his computer—no need to
print anything.

Reluctantly she allowed her eyes to finally rest on him and
again that little *frisson* of *something*. What was it about him
that did that to her? Was it because there was a watchful still-
ness about him that made her painfully self-conscious? When
he began walking towards her, her pulses leapt and she had
to make an effort not to take a couple of steps backwards.
Even with that slight limp, he moved with the grace of an
athlete, every muscle in his body honed to fine perfection.

She felt her breasts ache in a sudden unwelcome response
to his overpowering masculinity.

Dislikeable he might be, but he was, she conceded, drop
dead gorgeous. The black hair swept away from his face
threw into relentless emphasis the drama of his face. It would
be enough to send any woman into a dither, she concluded
uneasily, even one who disliked him and could smell him for
the heartbreaker he probably was from a mile away.

'I'll have a look at that heating and then I'll be off.' She
turned on her unsteady heel and headed for the boiler room
where, for a few minutes and some elementary twiddling, she
got the system going. When she turned round it was to find

him right behind her, leaning against the doorframe with his arms folded.

'You were right. Pretty easy.'

'Very. Now, if you don't mind…?'

'Why don't you stay for a drink?'

'I can't.' At least she could breathe when he wasn't looming over her like that.

He had followed her back out into the hall, where she was pulling on her jacket and seemed in a desperate rush to leave.

Theo was not accustomed to any woman being in a desperate rush to avoid his company. In fact, he had become adept at avoiding *theirs*. Before Elena, with variety spread before him like a moveable feast, he had sampled the wares and moved on. The physical pull towards a beautiful woman had always had temporary, limited appeal. It was the way he had liked it. Since Elena, the moveable feast had become a rude invasion of his privacy, but he had still been accustomed to having it there, to dealing with the necessity of avoiding it.

Something elemental kicked in now, in the face of a woman who was already making for the door as though he was a seriously infectious disease.

'Where are you going tonight?' he asked politely. The jacket was sizes too big for her and he wondered if it had belonged to her father. Or the blond man at the office with the over-developed protective streak.

'Oh.' Caught on the hop, Sophie looked at him for a few silent seconds, her face going redder by the minute as she tried to think of something fun she might be doing.

'Exciting nightclub somewhere?' Theo prompted silkily. He walked through to the kitchen and helped himself to a glass of wine. 'Cinema? Theatre, if there's one around here within striking distance? Maybe a restaurant?' He paused and sipped some of the wine. 'Or, of course, there's always the pub. Although you were quick to dispel the myth that all the locals do is frequent a pub and down pints of ale.'

'I suppose you think you're so clever,' Sophie told him in a shaking voice, to which he shrugged and walked towards the sitting room, leaving her with the option of either storming out in mid-tirade and looking like a coward, or else following him.

She followed to find him lounging on her sofa, thoroughly and infuriatingly calm.

'You might be some kind of writer. Who knows? Maybe you're even famous in that little circle you mix in, but that doesn't cut it with me!'

'What little circle?' Theo asked, curious to discover what image she had of his mysterious and fictional life.

'Oh, you know what I mean!'

'No, I don't.'

'That little circle of academics! Everyone sitting around, drinking wine and congratulating themselves on being so much smarter than the rest of the human race!'

There was a lot of insight in what she had just said, Theo thought, and it applied to his own circle of financiers and businessmen, the richest of the rich who could afford to relax on the Olympian summits of their own self-worth.

He watched her fume over the rim of his glass and nodded thoughtfully. 'You're right.'

'But don't think that you can swan in here and throw your weight around!' His words registered belatedly and she lapsed into silence. 'What did you just say?'

'I said you're right. There's a lot of self-righteous preening that takes place when wealthy, important people get together. It's fairly nauseating.'

'So you agree with me.'

'I agree with the concept, but not,' he said lazily, 'in so far as it applies to me.'

'Because…?' Sophie felt giddy. She took a couple of tentative steps into the sitting room and swore that she would be out of the cottage just as soon as he backed up his statement. She couldn't very well initiate this and then flounce off, could she? Not, she reminded herself piously, when he was her tenant, a small fact which, once again, she appeared to have forgotten.

'Because I happen to be a very modest man.' Quite a few, he admitted to himself, might disagree.

Something didn't sit right with that statement, but she had to admit that he had not been stingy in conceding her point. When he reiterated his offer of a glass of wine, she found herself accepting. She justified that easily on the grounds that it was just so nice being back in this sitting room, even if she had to share the space with a man like Theo Andreou. And, besides, her bank manager would appreciate her good manners.

He had drawn the curtains and the room was just how she loved it, bathed in the mellow glow of the standing lamp, with lots of shadows in the corners and the wind rattling against the window panes. Her father's books were ranged along one wall, housed in a bookcase that looked as old as the overhead beams.

'You hate this, don't you?'

Snapped back to the present, Sophie looked at him and frowned uncomfortably. 'Hate what?'

'Renting out this cottage to an arrogant bastard like me.'

Sophie dodged the description. 'It's been hard renting it out to you or to anyone.'

'But you had to because you needed the money.'

'Is this what you writers do?' she asked edgily. 'Cross-examine people and then use their reactions as fodder for books?'

'And is this what you do?' Theo asked coolly.

'What?'

'Categorise people?'

'I *do not categorise people*,' Sophie said. 'Well, not usually,' honesty compelled her to admit. 'Look, yes, you're right. I'm renting the cottage because I need the money and, no, I don't like doing it, as I said, because it's full of memories for me.'

'And what do you intend to do with it once your father's affairs have been sorted out? Was his expenditure as extravagant as you think?'

Sophie opened her mouth to tell him that her financial situation was none of his concern, and shut it again. She hadn't actually spoken to anyone about the mess that was her financial situation. Her bank manager knew and Robert, who had worked alongside her father off and on, a labour of love, as he told her, surely suspected the worst, but the other members of staff, Moira and Claire, wouldn't have a clue and it wouldn't have been fair to tell them. They were both in their fifties and had only ever worked on an occasional basis for her father, sometimes writing up complicated reports which would have meant nothing to them, or else generally tidying up in the wake of his discarded petri dishes and test tubes. They had indulged him and looked after him in the way an owner might look after a playful but lovable puppy, making sure that he ate, carting him off to their bridge groups and socials whenever they could.

He would never have let them in on the chaos of his accounts. He hadn't even let *her*, his own daughter, in on it! She had lived in blissful ignorance, doing her gap year in the neighbouring town, then on to university in Southampton, from which she had travelled home to see her father every fortnight. Only his death, interrupting the final leg of her teacher training, had woken her from her peaceful slumber and catapulted her into a confrontation with debt and money borrowed and money owing, all poured into her father's obsession with *discovering things*.

He had lived for the hope of *discovery*. Of *what exactly* he could only ever offer mysterious promises and the general assumption that in a world so full of complex life forms and even more complex diseases there was always something waiting to be discovered.

Over the years, Sophie had fondly considered his passion for *tinkering around* as a harmless hobby. He had been extremely bright and, having retired from his full-time job, it had kept him out of mischief.

Theo was looking at her with a shuttered expression. She knew that she would be safe from any saccharine-sweet expressions of sympathy from him. He would be blunt and he would probably reduce her to grinding her teeth in anger, but he wouldn't cluck his tongue and offer her a cup of tea. And he wouldn't insult her father's memory by asking how he could have been so irresponsible as to leave his only child to cope with his debts.

'Worse than that,' Sophie confessed.

Theo didn't say anything. He stood up and silently fetched the bottle of wine so that he could refill her glass.

Did he *need* any of this? Some stranger bawling out her troubles on his shoulder? Because he could smell a financial mess a mile off and he had smelled it big time in that office. It wasn't his problem and he didn't have to listen to anybody's tale of woe.

But a night spent reading through reports, updating files on his computer, downloading information on three companies he had his eye on, didn't hold much appeal on a rainy, cold October night behind God's back.

Theo looked at the downbent head consideringly before he handed her the glass of wine, topped up to confessional level.

He knew that the slightest hint of reluctance on his part to listen and she would be off. And she would make sure not to repeat the mistake. And, indeed, take away the fact that it was dark, rainy, cold and she had probably discovered yet one more IOU to add to the stockpile, and he knew that she would never have succumbed to any need to confide. She wasn't a confiding kind of girl.

What harm in indulging her need to talk? A village in the middle of nowhereland was not the place where confidantes could be easily located, not unless you wanted every member of the village to know your private business. Or at least so Theo assumed.

'Care to explain?' he asked, retreating to his chair and feeling suitably pleased with himself for actually bothering to listen to someone else's problems. Obeying doctor's orders, in fact! Doing this small good deed filled him with a bracing sense of virtue. 'You will find that I am very good at listening.'

CHAPTER THREE

SOPHIE looked at Theo's dark shuttered face and wondered where this strange urge to spill all her worries was coming from.

The man did not exude natural sympathy. In fact, she had to remind herself that he was a writer because he didn't embody any of the characteristics she associated with being in a creative profession.

But, right now, the world seemed to be on top of her shoulders. There seemed to be no end to the invoices and bills she was discovering by the minute and her father's cavalier approach to filing meant that there was the looming spectre of yet more debts waiting in the wings. She couldn't bring herself to discuss the situation with anyone she knew. Her friends from college would sympathise but really their heads would be somewhere else and, anyway, she hadn't seen them for ages.

And confiding in anyone in the village, even some of the people she had grown up with, would have been a huge mistake. She was determined to protect her father's reputation and not reveal the extent of his financial troubles.

Of course there was Robert. Sophie frowned at the thought of him. Theoretically he presented the perfect shoulder on which to cry, but for some reason she fought shy of confiding in him. To his credit, he didn't try and force her and a couple of times had even made it clear that he would be there for her, that however great the financial mess, he had savings and would bail her out.

It almost felt treacherous to be staring into Theo's enigmatic green eyes now, insanely tempted to pour her heart out. Robert would feel utterly betrayed.

But then Robert was too much of a fixture in her life. The advantage with Theo was that he would be gone in a matter of weeks and with him anything she said. There wouldn't even be a temptation to keep in touch with him because she didn't particularly care for him. In a sense, that, too, made it easier.

'You've listened to a lot of other people's problems, have you?' Sophie asked with a wry smile.

'It's not usually something I encourage.'

'I thought you said that you were a good listener.'

'I am. Which isn't to say that I encourage people to pour out their problems to me.'

'Thank you for telling me that. It's just the right thing to make me feel at ease.' Extraordinarily, she *did* feel stupidly relaxed. 'Why don't you like people pouring out their problems to you?'

'Because most people like advice, they like solutions. They want to be told what their next difficult step might be and no one can advise anyone else on what they should do to sort themselves out. So, to avoid being called upon to do that, I prefer to refrain from putting myself in the firing line, so to speak.'

'Sometimes it just helps to talk,' Sophie said slowly.

'And, as I said, I'm willing to listen.' He had never talked about Elena. At her funeral, he had been surrounded by sympathetic well-wishers. He had been positively drowning under the torrent of well-meaning compassion. But at no point had he felt inclined to talk to anyone about what he was going through. Not even his mother could penetrate the defence system he'd erected like a steel cordon around his emotions.

His emotions, like everything else in his life, he could take care of by himself.

'Didn't you know that your father was in debt? Is that the problem?'

'Part of it,' Sophie admitted. 'Do you mind if I help myself to another glass of wine? I'm not accustomed to discussing my private life with other people.'

Theo felt a strange sense of satisfaction that he had got it right about this aspect of her personality. It seemed to him an almost masculine trait because, in his experience, there wasn't a woman alive who didn't enjoy discussing every small facet of whatever happened to be flitting through her mind.

It was reassuring to think of his landlady in those terms. Masculine, brusque, quick to bristle, never mind the stubby girlish plaits or the soft pink of her cheeks as she glanced away from him.

'There's nothing less private than a financial mess,' Theo said dryly.

'Why do you say that?'

'Because it always needs cleaning up and it's almost impossible to hide the cleaning up tools once you set to work.'

'Don't say that!'

'Why not?'

'Because I don't want my father's reputation to be ruined. I don't want him to be remembered as the man who left a mess for his daughter to sort out. I don't want to be an object of pity.'

'No.' Theo could certainly understand that one. 'So how big is the mess?'

'I honestly don't know where to begin. Dad was the most disorganised person in the world. He has notes scribbled on pieces of paper in places no one would think of looking. Just yesterday I found a file stuffed at the back of the sofa in the sitting room above the office.'

'Which your father used…?'

'Oh, when he was very busy into the night reviewing something or other. Which is another problem. I don't actually understand a lot of what's in his files so I don't know whether to bin them or not. Robert's been good helping me go through them, but there are just so many!'

'Tell me about Robert.'

'Why?'

'How does he fit into the dynamics?'

'He worked with my father, off and on, so to speak. He's a trained pharmacist as well. I think he saw my dad as something of a mentor and, in the absence of a son to carry on the profession, Dad was pleased to have Robert tagging along over the past few years, especially as I've been away a lot of the time, going to university and doing my teacher training.'

'So the two of you go back a long way?'

'I guess so,' Sophie said in a guarded voice.

Theo's curiosity cranked into gear and, with it, his age-old talent for reading members of the opposite sex. He had always been able to sense what the slight change in body posture meant, the barely noticeable shift in tone, the quick glance. It was a talent that had spent the past eighteen months getting rusty.

'Why do I sense a certain reticence on your part to discuss him? Normally when it comes to women that usually implies a relationship there and more often than not sex is involved. Is it?'

Sophie stared at Theo, stupefied.

'Just an observation,' he murmured, looking down at his empty glass and lazily reaching for the bottle of wine which Sophie had thoughtfully placed on the table in front of him. A thread of adrenaline seared through his blood.

The highly charged emotion of winning an important deal or even taking a life or death risk with his life, as he had done on the dangerous black run a few weeks back, faded into insignificance as he looked at her face.

He felt shamefully but guiltily alive. He knew that if circumstances had been different, if he had been in London, he would have resented her for awakening his ability to feel, but down here things seemed different. He had a different persona, just a man caught in a bubble in which reality was not much of an intrusion. He had no demands from the people he knew, no colleagues or clients to inspire, no familiar faces staring at him from the sidelines of his predictable run of social gatherings, most of which he ignored but a few of which he roused himself to attend.

No, here he was a mystery author who had no past and no future. There were no expectations on his shoulders. In a few weeks he would pack his bags, get his driver down and return to his normal life.

In the meantime he could be whoever the hell he wanted to be.

Anonymity had never smelled sweeter.

'Financial problems usually involve more than one player. Hence my curiosity as to where this Robert character fits in. He probably knows a hell of a lot more than you think about your father's debts. Are you sure they're all to do with his work? If he and this boy were close, you might want to consider that he may have been forking out money to him, treating him like a son who might need bailing out now and again… Or maybe this so-called old friend of yours has been taking money out of the till, hence his enthusiasm to help you out now. One way of making sure that he gets his hands on anything that involves him…'

'What on earth are you talking about?' Sophie laughed shortly, allowing herself not to be poleaxed by his provocative suggestions about Robert. It was just good not to be lying in bed worrying and the fact that she didn't like him much was even better for her because it meant that she could be herself. If he had disliked her attitude so much he would have left the cottage within minutes of being subjected to her first tirade but in some part of her she knew that he would just have written it off as unconventional behaviour and, from what she could see, he looked as though he exhibited quite a bit of that himself.

'And how do you happen to know about *financial players*, whatever *that* means?'

'I know about a lot of things,' Theo said smoothly. 'Certainly enough to be highly suspicious when it comes to anything to do with money.'

Sophie opened her mouth to level something sarcastic at that sweeping piece of self-flattery, but thought better of it. She realised that he probably *did* know about a lot of things. 'There are no *players*,' she found herself saying, smiling in fact at the thought of her father being some kind of crazed, criminal puppet master with accomplices lurking behind every door. Or, even more comical, good-natured Robert cunningly sneaking money from the till.

'What's so funny?'

'The thought of my father engaged in underhand wheeler-dealing. And Robert isn't some kind of dastardly accomplice who's stitched up the books.' She sighed heavily. 'No, the truth is much simpler. My father loved experimenting. He was born to live life in a lab. It used to drive my mum mad. He experimented and wrote his notes and ordered his substances and there are records of some and records of others and paperwork that keeps popping up from every nook and cranny. That's what we're doing at the office—trying to go through all of it and tie it up into bundles. Problem is, there's paperwork in this house as well. I know it. And in the flat above the office. And Lord knows where else! And Robert is just trying to help me put it all in order.'

'How thoughtful of him,' Theo murmured. The woman must be half blind not to spot the fact that the man was more than halfway to being in love with her.

He looked at her. Really looked at her. The slant of her body as she leaned forward in the chair. The combat trousers, he had to admit, looked a little sexy on her, probably because she was so slender, and under the cream jumper he was very much aware of the soft mounds of her breasts. Suddenly and painfully aware. After such a long haul of self-imposed celibacy, fierce heat slammed through Theo's body like a sledgehammer. He crossed his legs, doing his best to ensure that his suddenly obvious physical response wasn't visible.

He was aware that she was telling him about her father, about his habits. She obviously hadn't heard his sarcastic rejoinder about Robert and, for the time being, Theo was more than happy to listen to her talk, anything to give his body an opportunity to get back to normal.

He tried to conjure up Elena's face. No luck. The urgency of his response was too powerful. He placed one hand flat on his thigh and fidgeted uncomfortably.

'Are you all right?' Sophie asked, concerned. 'Am I boring you?'

'Not at all,' Theo muttered. His eyes strayed down to her thighs. She was sitting on her hands and when she leaned forward like that... He just knew that she wasn't wearing a bra.

He just managed to control the groan that threatened to escape.

'I could go...'

'No!' He waved her down, even though she hadn't stood up. 'No. Look, why don't you stay and have some dinner with me? There's stuff in the fridge. Catherine has been very diligent about...making sure that I don't go hungry. At any point.'

'I don't know...' She thought of the meal for one waiting back at the flat for her. Robert had invited her out to dinner, but she had refused the offer on the grounds of exhaustion. And she really *had* been exhausted an hour ago. Where it had gone was a mystery.

'Okay,' she said, making her mind up. 'But I won't stay for very long. It's been a tiring week.' She stood up, expecting him to follow suit.

'You...go ahead... I'll join you in the kitchen in a short while. I'm just going to...have a quick shower...'

'Now?'

'Seize the moment,' Theo said. He waited until she had left the room before heading to his bedroom, taking the stairs and exhaling a long sigh of relief when he was safely ensconced in the bedroom.

He hadn't felt this horny since he was a teenager and he was far from proud of himself. The cool water took a while to take effect but at least he felt in control once again when he strolled downstairs to find her in the kitchen and the table set.

Sophie looked up at him and her heart skipped a beat. His hair was still damp and he had changed into some beige trousers and a baggy white T-shirt that brought out the drama of his colouring.

'You haven't let me forget that this is your cottage,' Theo said, fetching another bottle of wine from the fridge and pouring them both fresh glasses, 'but it still seems strange to walk into the kitchen and find the table set.' He wished to God that he hadn't asked her to stay. Now that he was back in control of himself, he could feel a bitter resentment simmering inside him at the way his body had betrayed him. And the whole domestic scene laid out before him, while it was hardly her fault, only made matters worse.

What was he doing? His body was responding like a dog on heat to a woman whose personality left him cold.

'It would seem odd to me not to set it,' Sophie replied. She turned away hurriedly and began prodding the chicken, which she had transferred from a casserole dish to a frying pan. 'I apologise for making myself at home…'

'In your own home?' Theo laughed shortly, watching how her slim shoulders stiffened.

'While there's a tenant in the cottage, it's no longer my *home*. It's just bricks and mortar to look after so that no problems arise with the fabric of the house.' She reluctantly turned around and leaned against the counter top, arms folded. 'Perhaps this wasn't such a good idea,' she continued awkwardly. 'You should have eaten your chicken on your own and I should have gone out to dinner with Robert.'

Theo afforded her a swift look but she wasn't looking at him. She was frowning and staring into the distance. He had an insane impulse to drag her back to the here and now, which was dinner with *him*. 'You should be careful of that man,'

Theo murmured and at first he wasn't sure if she had even taken in what he had said but, sure enough, after a few seconds Sophie looked at him in open astonishment.

The familiar anger flooded into her and she had never been happier to feel an unpleasant emotion. Earlier on there had been moments of breathless confusion that had had her floundering and uncertain. She glared at him.

'Do I need to ask *why* or will you tell me anyway?'

'Okay, he may not be a crook, but I've met men like him before…'

'Oh. And would that be in the fascinating world of literature?'

Theo ignored the interruption. 'They're insecure, hesitant, desperate for a bit of love. They're the ones who marry the first woman they meet so that they can retire from the headache of the chase. Basically, they're losers.'

'That's the most ridiculous thing I've ever heard in my life! Robert isn't a *loser*.'

'Sadly, men like that,' Theo mused, disregarding her heated objections, 'usually go for a strong-willed woman, much like yourself…'

'I'm not even going to *pretend* to be listening.' She turned and stuck the rice into the microwave, pushing the numbers hard to drown out the sound of his voice. Not that he was saying anything. At the moment. He was looking at her. She could feel his eyes boring through her top and the sensation was like having her breasts touched by him, a feathery soft caress that made her redden.

For some reason she wished she had worn a bra, but then she hadn't expected to be staying on for dinner—just fixing the heating and clearing off—and it was comfortable not having her breasts constrained. Although she was slight in build, she was not flat chested. The opposite, in fact. She now felt the weight of her generous breasts bouncing under the loose jumper, swaying as she dished out the food.

'Dinner,' she said flatly, nodding to his plate and sitting down at the kitchen table opposite him.

'And the end of our conversation, I take it?'

Sophie watched him, hunkered over his plate, eating the chicken with his fork, every inch the kind of alpha male who could walk into a room and have the ladies swooning. She would have to be as thick as a plank of wood not to realise that the man's massive ego and staggering self-assurance would have come from the power he probably exerted over the opposite sex. Did he think that his extraordinary looks somehow qualified him to be a judge of what made other people tick? Whatever he said, she couldn't believe that his contact with the rest of the world was particularly huge, never mind how many books he had had published in the past. Writing was a solitary profession. Yes, if he wrote real adventures about real people, then he would have to interview them, but after that he would be on his own, transcribing. Transcribing at a desk somewhere in London certainly didn't qualify him to offer advice on one of her closest male friends.

She wondered whether he assumed that she must be completely ignorant of the opposite sex, living in this backwater as she did.

Suddenly, Sophie felt an unusual protective urge towards Robert. She thought of his little kindnesses recently and bitterly resented Theo's sweeping assumption that he could insult the man without compunction.

'You can say what you like about Robert, but he's gentle and kind and considerate. In fact…' she allowed a few seconds of silence to stress the importance of what she was going to say '…he's even offered to help *bail me out* of this financial mess…'

'Really,' Theo drawled.

'Really.' Sophie shot him a smug little smile, which he greeted by raising his eyebrows in apparent amusement.

'Maybe he just wants to get you into bed and buttering you up with an offer he knows you'll probably refuse seems the quickest way.'

Sophie recovered quickly. 'Maybe that's it. Although maybe I wouldn't need buttering up to get into bed with him…' She gave a shrug which she hoped displayed the wealth of worldly wisdom which was definitely not at her disposal. Whether it was the wine or a combination of the wine and the dangerously intrusive conversation, she was beginning to feel heady. She was twenty-six years old and she couldn't remember ever having a conversation like this before. The boys in her circle, most of whom were doing post grad courses, would never have dreamt of challenging her in this way. She didn't know whether she liked it or not. And she didn't know whether she liked the excitement that was fizzing in her veins as she met his stare. If someone had asked her what she was eating, she would have had to think about it, even though she had been the one to dish it up.

'Somehow he strikes me as a bit too tame for a woman like you. Unless, of course, you like the role of dominatrix,' Theo mused aloud, finishing his chicken and shoving the plate away from him. He leaned back into his chair and looked at her steadily. There was a little drop of sauce from the chicken on her chin, by her mouth, and he allowed himself the rogue thought of wondering what she would do if he covered the three steps towards her, bent down and licked it off.

Guilt followed hard on the heels of the wayward image, but there was none of that savage longing he had had in the past to hold on to the image of Elena. The steady drumming of rain outside, the bursts of wind clawing against the window panes, was like a lullaby, easing his tortured conscience, leaving him free to indulge himself in the sight of her playing with the food on her plate.

'You've got some sauce on your chin.'

'Oh!' Sophie wiped it off and licked her finger. For some strange reason, Theo found the innocent gesture intensely erotic. The erection he had put to rest earlier on was once more reminding him that he was still a man and one with very real physical needs.

'Mind you, if you don't really know whether the man actually wants you or not, then his technique can't be very persuasive…' Theo murmured, returning to the conversation and enjoying the faint flush of colour that spread along her cheekbones. There was nothing masculine about *that* reaction, he thought. In fact, it was very, very feminine.

Before his body decided to do something of its own volition, he stood up and began clearing away the plates, insisting she stay put while he tidied.

'I'm a twenty-first century man,' he said, which was enough to make him grin. *Dinosaur* was one of the labels an ex-girl-friend from years back had once told him and certainly, however much he was in favour of equality of the sexes in the workplace, he still saw almost every chore to do with the house as something firmly planted in a woman's domain. In fact, if he thought about it, he really couldn't remember the last time he had ever done what he was now in the process of doing, namely clearing the dishes from a table after he had shared a meal with a woman.

In fact, thinking even harder on the matter, he realised that sharing a meal with a woman anywhere other than a restaurant or, at a push, her place, was not something that had ever been on his agenda. Women fussing in his kitchen had always made him feel slightly uneasy. Until Elena. Although…

Had she ever cooked for him? No—not enough time to enjoy the pleasures of domesticity before tragedy had taken her away. Their relationship had been frozen in the courtship stage.

Before he could travel down the usual inexorable path, he realised that Sophie was saying something about his twenty-first century man observation and in a particularly acerbic tone of voice, he realised.

'What am I doing?' he demanded, temporarily distracted. He brandished one plate in his hand and looked meaningfully at the sink.

'You're putting your dirty plate into the sink and you've been polite enough to take mine as well. I wouldn't,' she added with scathing sarcasm, 'be too hasty to enter any *Man of the Year* competitions based on that…'

Before she could continue, Theo had swept round to face her and leant over her, bracing himself on the arms of her chair. He was so close to her, in fact, that she could see the golden specks in his eyes, was horribly aware of the thickness and length of his eyelashes, acutely conscious of the sexy contours of his mouth.

She was also very *very* conscious of her own body and the way it was shrieking in response. Her nipples, grazing the thick cotton of her jumper, had tightened into buds and every part of her seemed to be melting.

She could breathe him in. His uniquely clean male scent filled her nostrils and she blinked away the temptation to sigh and close her eyes.

'And, in your opinion, what would qualify me to enter that *Man of the Year* competition…?' Theo drawled. His eyes dropped to her heaving breasts and he hurriedly fastened them safely back on her face.

'*Not* an ability to move a dish from one part of the kitchen to another…'

Theo grinned and then laughed softly under his breath. 'What, then?'

Their eyes met and Sophie was sickeningly transfixed. Her heart was beating like a drum inside her, reverberating in her head and making her pulse race. In a minute she half expected to lose the power of speech completely.

If he would only give her a little more breathing room, she might be able to gather herself into the coherent, fairly unflappable young woman she had always considered herself to be. As it was, she could feel her face getting hotter and hotter and probably redder and redder as well.

He must have read her mind because, to her intense relief, he pushed himself away and fetched two mugs down from the cupboard. In her flurry of nerves, Sophie could hardly focus on resenting him for knowing his way around her house as well as she did.

Instead, clearing her throat, she told him that she had to be getting along.

'I apologise if I made you feel awkward by stepping on your toes about your boyfriend…'

'Robert is *not* my boyfriend! And, anyway, you didn't make me feel *awkward*. I'm not completely green when it comes to men, you know.'

'No?'

'No,' Sophie said firmly, before he decided to question her on the subject. She wouldn't put it past him. His lines between interested and downright rude seemed to be very blurry.

She stood up, making sure to keep a healthy distance away from him. For a kitchen that had always seemed more than big enough, it suddenly felt claustrophobically small. 'Shall I give you a hand with those dishes?' she asked politely. She was pretty sure that he would leave them for Annie to do in the morning but reverting to her professional role of landlady went some distance to rescuing her from her muddled confusion.

'And risk giving you an even bigger reason to accuse me of not being the perfect example of Modern Man…?' Theo murmured, dragging a smile out of her. He folded his arms and leaned against the counter. He might, actually, wash the damned dishes. 'I'm still interested in hearing your definition…'

'Oh, it's the same as any other woman's…'

'Some women like their men to be men…'

Sophie edged imperceptibly towards the kitchen door. 'Are you sure you don't mean *cavemen*?' she asked caustically. 'These days women like men who share everything, from household duties to bringing up the kids. They like men who aren't afraid to cry and who are willing to admit when they've made a mistake…'

Theo struggled not to laugh. 'Not all women…' he pointed out, moving towards her. He knew that he was flirting outrageously and it felt good. Reality was happening somewhere else but, here and now, there was just this. Feeling like a human being after months spent in a wilderness. He wasn't about to forget that the wilderness was still there, waiting for him, but he could snatch this feeling of normality and enjoy it for a short while.

This woman was nothing to him and never could be. She was too forthright, too abrasive and too damned *unpredictable*. In the blink of an eye she went from being erotically feminine to aggressively unappealing.

Right now, one of the plaits was coming undone, which he had to admit looked quite cute.

Spotting his eyes on her hair, Sophie dragged the elastic

bands off and ran her fingers through the blunt blonde mane. Plaits were no good. Not when she was trying hard to hold on to her sang-froid.

'Maybe not the ones *you* mix with…' Sophie retorted. She wondered what sort of women he mixed with and came up with an assortment of choices, all stunningly beautiful and probably very tall. A drop dead gorgeous man in a glamorous field of work and with a good bank balance, if his ability to meet the rent was anything to go by, would want a woman who could match him for style and looks.

'Can you truthfully tell me that you prefer a sensitive man who gets excited at cooking the evening meal and weeps during sad movies?'

Sophie felt her mouth twitch and she stared down at her feet.

'Maybe,' Theo murmured slowly, 'it works if you want a man who can sit with you in the evenings and do some cross stitch in between gossiping about the latest reality show on TV…'

Sophie was not going to give in to the temptation to laugh. She reminded herself of his ability to be as arrogant as hell, not to mention targeting her personal life and asking questions that were way out of line. Because he also had a wicked sense of humour when he chose, it just made him all the more infuriating.

She schooled her expression into one of thoughtful agreement. 'Yes, companionship is always wonderful…' she mused. 'Obviously the cross stitching is taking it a bit too far, but a man who can cook—well, actually, I don't think you'll find too many women who would run screaming in the opposite direction from that…'

'Maybe you're right,' Theo drawled lazily. 'Maybe it's the women I've mixed with. They have fed me the illusion that what turned them on was strength of character…'

He flicked the tea towel in his hand over one shoulder and began to walk in her direction. Sophie very nearly yelped in sudden alarm.

She spun round on her heel, before her legs could let her down by turning to lead, and headed straight for the front door. She spoke with her back to him, rambling on about strength of character having nothing to do with whether a man was sensitive or not. She knew that he was right behind her, would be seeing her to the door so that he could lock it behind her. She reached the door and grasped the door knob just as Theo drew even with her.

There was a lingering scent of some light floral perfume on her. Theo could smell it very faintly. And her hair, no longer in plaits, was a mass of tiny waves falling softly around her face.

Typically, she was gabbling on in an argumentative manner about something or other, like an irate little terrier snapping angrily at nothing in particular. Theo grinned down at her just as she raised her eyes and she glared, on the verge of continuing her running disgruntled monologue.

'If women want the sensitive, culinary type of man, then can I give you some advice…? Men want women who don't rant all the time…'

Theo thought she might explode on the spot. This time he couldn't help himself. He flung back his head and laughed and, God, did it feel good.

Sophie, rendered speechless, stared at him open-mouthed and was still staring at him when he finally sobered up.

'Course,' he murmured in a dangerously soft voice, 'there *is* one foolproof way to stop a woman in mid-tirade…'

She should have sensed it but, even when he leant against the doorframe and lowered his head to hers, the feel of his mouth against hers was shockingly unexpected. She gasped and was driven back as he kissed her deeper, harder, with the urgency of a man denied physical contact for too long.

His body was pressed against hers and she was mindlessly aware of his erection. Her breasts were crushed against his chest, painful and sensitive and yearning for him to pull up her jumper and lave them with his tongue.

The full inappropriate horror of the situation hit her seconds after it hit him and Theo was the first to pull back, enraged with himself and filled with sudden savage self-disgust.

Worse than the lapse in his self-control was the knowledge that he had enjoyed every minute of that kiss, had wanted to do more.

'Go…' he rasped and Sophie frantically yanked open the door, shaking like a leaf.

He was aware of her leaving and knew that he had locked the door behind her. Somehow he found himself in his bedroom where, for once, his drift off to sleep was not preceded by a couple of hours on his laptop computer.

Events, whatever you wanted to call it, had taken him by surprise and now he would need to figure out what to do. Because if there was one thing Theo did not welcome in his life it was surprise. With surprises, in his experience, always came an element of the nasty and nasty was something he would ruthlessly excise from his life, whatever the cost…

CHAPTER FOUR

SOPHIE thought that it was a sad reminder of her man-less existence that the memory of that fleeting kiss haunted her over the next three days. She couldn't understand how it had happened. She barely knew the man and disliked a fair bit of what she *did* know, and yet she couldn't remember ever being more turned on by a kiss. Just thinking about it afterwards made her feel giddy.

Of course it wouldn't take long for that ridiculous sensation to fade away and she had planned on keeping out of his way as much as she could to ensure that the fading process took as little time as possible. Besides, seeing him again would be embarrassing for both of them. She might have been shocked at what had happened but his reaction had been a lot more extreme. He had looked angry and disgusted with himself and had hustled her out of the cottage with such speed that she was surprised she had made it out of the door in one piece. She didn't know what that had been about but she was sharp enough to realise that he would probably be even happier than her not to be reminded of the brief physical encounter.

Which was why she found herself staring at the note on her desk with such dismay.

'They can't do this!' she protested to Robert, who was tackling a stack of papers with the aid of a chocolate bar. Moira and Claire had both left for the evening, Christmas shopping before the crowds descended, and, Sophie suspected, the temptation to do something a little less relentless and a little more rewarding than plough through innumerable files. She couldn't blame them. There was nothing more conducive to killing the Christmas spirit than the contemplation of yet more paperwork that had to be matched up and puzzled over. Only Robert remained loyal to the cause. His pace of work was slow, but he was thorough and uncomplaining. Sophie had realised some time back that she could ask for little more.

'They can and they will,' he now said, linking his fingers on his stomach and looking at her. 'It may have escaped you but this part of the world doesn't rank right up there with London, Tokyo and New York...'

'Which isn't to say that the electricity board can plunge us all into darkness virtually in the middle of winter!' Sophie protested.

'For a few hours, Soph! I think we can all manage to do without electricity between eight and one tomorrow! Course, we won't be able to work here,' he pointed out, casting a jaundiced eye around him. 'This place is like a dungeon without the lights on.'

Sophie's mind was already racing ahead. Would they have notified Theo of the power cut? Probably not. She had had her mail redirected to her office address as soon as the cottage had been let. It would be her responsibility to let her tenant know the situation.

Which meant facing the man.

'Why don't you and I bunk off tomorrow? Go do a little

Christmas shopping… You could do with a break. I'll treat you to lunch…'

Sophie, staring off into the distance, wondered how she could avoid the uncomfortable task of calling in on Theo. She shuddered to think what his reaction would be on seeing her on his doorstep. Or, rather, on *her* doorstep.

'Hello? Is anybody there?'

Sophie registered that Robert had been saying something to her but, for the life of her, she didn't know what precisely, and her expression must have given her away for the smile dropped and he reddened.

'I'm sorry, Robert. What were you saying?'

'I was saying that you need to take a break from all this, Sophie.' He made a sweeping gesture towards the paper overload swamping the surfaces of the desks and quite a bit of the ground as well. 'This stuff isn't important, not really, and you're getting consumed…'

'The quicker I go through it, the faster it'll be finished and I can get back to finishing my teacher training.'

'And leave here? The cottage? Everything…?'

'Just for a while…'

'What if you literally *can't afford to leave*?'

'What do you mean?'

'I mean, if there's no money in the till, you might have to abandon your course or sell the cottage. Now, I know you don't want to…'

'To be having this conversation…' She stood up and slung on her jumper, then her coat. Her life was in turmoil now, but she pinned her hopes on the future sorting it out, smoothing over the problems. She didn't want to confront the grim possibility that nothing might be sorted out and she might, just might, be left picking up pieces for longer than she anticipated. 'I can't afford to have this conversation,' she continued, grabbing her bag and stuffing the power cut note inside it. 'I can't afford to think that everything is going to start falling apart around me…'

'Which it needn't…' Robert had leapt to his feet and was rallying around her like a diligent sheepdog rounding up a wayward stray sheep. Sophie glanced up from where she was now trying to locate the office keys in her capacious bag.

'Oh, Robert, not this again. I know you feel sorry for me…'

'Is that what you think?'

'Well…yes…' She laughed nervously because he was standing quite close to her and there was a shy nervousness about him that was making her feel a little confused. 'I do, as a matter of fact. I mean, we've known each other off and on over the years and I don't suppose you ever expected this situation to happen. I mean, that's why you've been so kind to me, isn't it…' Keys located, she closed her fist around them and shoved her hands into her deep coat pockets.

'Why do you imagine that I worked with your father for such a long time…? Off and on…?' He reached out and stroked her hair. Sophie's eyes widened. If she could have commanded the ground to open up and swallow her whole, she would have. This was certainly a week for shocks. First Theo and now this—pleasant, background Robert declaring…what? She resisted the urge to laugh. Somehow she didn't imagine that he would appreciate the gesture. He was, as Theo had hinted, vulnerable and probably insecure around women.

'Because you liked him?' Sophie offered hopefully, and Robert shook his head.

'Sure I liked him…' There was genuine wistfulness in his voice. 'And I enjoyed his company, his enthusiasm, but I also enjoyed hanging around here so that I could see *you*…'

'Me?' she squeaked.

'Which is why I want to help bail you out of this mess if you need to be bailed out…I don't want to sound pessimistic, but…' He allowed a few seconds of silence to elapse, during which Sophie had ample opportunity to dwell on the most pessimistic scenario he could come up with. 'What if, at the end of this exercise, the only thing you discover is a mountain of debt? You can sell the cottage, but there's still a mortgage on it.'

'How do you know that?'

'How does anyone around here know anything?' Robert answered with a wry grimace. 'The birds on the trees… But what I'm saying,' he carried on, considering his words carefully, 'is that I've saved enough for you to carry on with your course, to do what you want to do…'

'And you would lend me the money?' Sophie asked dubiously, 'even though I wouldn't be able to pay you back for a while…?'

'I wouldn't have to lend you the money,' he said patiently and he shook his head when she continued to stare at him in baffled silence. 'What I'm saying is… Would you consider marrying me?' He laughed nervously and grabbed her hand, tugging it away from the warm protection of her coat pocket.

'Marry you?'

'I know we haven't got a conventional relationship…'

'Robert, we haven't *got* a relationship!'

'Which is something I want to remedy…I would really like to settle down now, start a family.'

'But we've only ever been just good friends, Robert…'

'It doesn't have to stay that way. I'm attracted to you, Soph…'

'No, you're not!'

'I am! What can I say to convince you?'

For the second time in about as many days, Sophie was caught utterly off guard. One minute he was standing there, looking at her earnestly. The next minute he had managed to close the gap between them without her noticing and his lips were on hers, exploring her open-mouthed surprise.

Like a badly dubbed movie, there was a couple of seconds of delay between Sophie being aware of what was going on and reacting to it, but when she did react it was with some vigour.

She pulled back, trembling, and stared at him crossly.

'Okay!' He held up his hands and smiled crookedly at her. 'But think about it, Sophie. Promise me you'll think about it…' At the door, he paused and turned to look at her. 'I just think we're both ready for a committed relationship. I know I am and, in a way, your financial situation just seems like fate putting us together. I could help you out and we could have a great life together.'

'Robert…'

He placed one finger over his mouth, willing her to be silent. 'I'm going to be away for the next couple of weeks, anyway. Dad's not very well, so I'm going to go up to give Mum a hand. I was going to leave it till the beginning of next week, but I'll go tomorrow, give you time on your own to think about what I've asked…You know, Mum would love you… She's desperate for some grandchildren. But, anyway, when I get back, maybe we could go out? Discuss things…?'

He didn't really give her time to answer that, which was just as well since Sophie, stunned into silence, couldn't think of anything to say.

She wondered how she could have missed all those signs that Theo seemed to have picked up after a couple of minutes. Robert's mum wasn't desperate—*he* was!

She would have spent the rest of the evening worrying about that. Instead, paying a visit to Theo seemed less of a nightmare and more of a distraction from having to think about what Robert had said. She found herself heading directly to the cottage shortly after Robert had gone and she had locked up for the night.

It was only when she glimpsed the glow of the lights that had been switched on that she faltered. Well, of course he was going to be in! Where else would he be likely to be? Now that she was here, the sickening thought, which she had conveniently sidelined, rose to the surface with monstrous ease—how was he going to react when he saw her? She hoped that he would follow her lead and pretend that nothing had happened, but what if he slammed the door in her face?

Sophie knew with unerring instinct that she was not physically Theo's type. She didn't know why he had kissed her; maybe isolation had generated an irresistible urge and she had just happened to be around at the time. He had known that she would respond because what woman wouldn't? The man was gorgeous. But he had realised his mistake almost as soon as he had committed it. Because she was no sex siren. She was just average Sophie Scott. Should she be grateful for Robert's proposal? It had taken her unawares, but should she at least consider going out with him on a date? A real date? With possible commitment at the end of the road? Robert might not set her ablaze but at least he wouldn't reject her with obvious insulting distaste after one kiss.

From the small study, where Theo had been staring at his computer screen, willing it to work its usual magic and suck him in, he glanced up at the sound of the doorbell.

The study was in an advantageous position. Since the house was very old, it was highly doubtful whether it had been specifically designed for the purpose, but the study permitted an unobscured angled view of the front door. From where Theo was sitting, and with the porch light shining directly down on to her, he could easily make out Sophie's thoughtful expression.

Instead of getting to his feet, Theo pushed himself back from the desk and continued to look at her, fingers steepled under his chin.

He had known that she would come back. Sooner or later. If she hadn't, then he would have sought her out under some pretext or other, but he was pleased that the necessity to do that hadn't arisen. Active pursuit would not have sat quite right with him.

But now...

He wondered what she would think if she knew what was going through his head right now. After his performance a couple of days ago, chances were high that she would belt him. He had, he admitted, not behaved in a very gentlemanly manner. In fact, he had committed the ultimate sin as far as a woman was concerned—he had succumbed to a physical situation only to reel away in disgust, and Sophie would not have known that his disgust had been aimed at himself. She would have felt insulted and mortified. Especially as she had responded so eagerly to him.

The doorbell rang again and he saw her stare upwards impatiently, one foot tapping, hands thrust into her coat pockets.

With a little sigh, Theo stood up and headed out towards the front door.

He took his time, giving himself an opportunity to talk himself out of his decision. The past three days had not been good for Theo. In fact, dealing with the long months of grieving had almost been easier. At least grief was a known quantity, an emotion he could understand and deal with accordingly. He could lose himself in reckless abandonment on the ski slopes and twice against the unforgiving face of a perpendicular cliff face. He could take financial risks and savour the illusion it gave him of being alive. Of course, in the end, he had always returned to his silent mourning but even that, he now acknowledged, had a quality of predictability about it.

But succumbing to ten seconds of physical connection with another human being had catapulted Theo into a state of unacceptable confusion.

For three days he hadn't been able to concentrate. The dull background noise of his computer, once such a comforting sound, had thrown him into a mindless reverie in which he'd dwelled on the way her lips had felt as they had touched his, the feel of her soft skin crushed against his hard body, the sensation of his own body flaring out of control.

It wasn't going to do. Nor did he intend to dwell on it as a problem which had landed on his doorstep and lacked a solution. Every problem had a solution and every situation could be dealt with.

He had dealt with Elena's death and he could certainly deal with the sudden war raging now between his body and his brain.

Theo had looked at the situation with the cold detachment of someone intent on analysing and staring down a dilemma.

He had responded to the woman and he wasn't a fool. He knew why. Removed from his normal environment, indeed from the routine of his life, he had behaved in a manner that was extraordinary given the iron control he had maintained over himself over the past year and a half. Without the eyes of the world upon him, he had broken away from his normal pattern of behaviour. This was excusable.

But facing the reality of his motivation had done very little to staunch the surge of inappropriate lust he had felt every time he thought about her.

That was something he was less certain about. Why *her*? There had been many a more enticing woman beckoning before and he had managed to ignore them all. Indeed, they had irritated the hell out of him. So why finally crack with someone like his landlady? A woman who was annoying, abrasive and not particularly headturning at that?

Again he arrived at the conclusion that it was all to do with the circumstance in which he now found himself, far removed from the reality of London and his working life and with no links to anyone he personally knew. Freedom to behave how he wanted with the comforting blanket of anonymity around his shoulders.

He was *feeling* for the first time in well over a year and Theo, recognising that with dispassionate honesty, treated the unforeseen situation in much the same way as he had dealt with the horror of Elena's unpredictable death. He was a man of action and he would take action. If his body was telling him that it was finally stirring into life, then he would obey the demands of his body. The fact that the unlikely recipient of his awakening was a woman he would never have looked at twice before was in itself a good thing. There was no risk of entanglement. They were physically attracted to one another but beyond that there was nothing. She might even dislike him, strange though the concept was.

The thought of her actively disliking him was peculiarly jarring. He relegated it to the back of his mind and focused on the immediate prospect of seduction, free from questions about a future and unconcerned with questions about the past. A moment in time and a step forward for him.

Concerns about Sophie's compliance in this general scheme of things barely crossed Theo's mind. He knew, with the instincts of a deeply sexual man, that she was attracted to him, had enjoyed him touching her, had wanted more. For him, that was enough. He had no problem being a moment in time for her. Indeed, he would have had it no other way.

He pulled open the door and Sophie was greeted with a crooked smile that made her heart do a little somersault inside her. She had half expected him not to let her in but he stood aside and, after a moment's hesitation, Sophie brushed past him before turning to face him in the flagstoned hall.

'An unexpected surprise,' Theo drawled. He gently shut the door, noticing that she wasn't removing her coat. 'Would you care for something to drink?'

'No, thank you. I've just come to tell you that there is going to be a power cut tomorrow. Only for a few hours, but I'm afraid you won't be able to use your computer. Or anything else, for that matter. Well, anything that relies on current, which is pretty much everything.' Sophie smiled nervously while he continued to watch her through narrowed eyes. She wanted to edge towards the door but he had stayed put right in front of it. She knew that he wasn't trying to hem her in. In fact, he seemed perfectly relaxed, almost *friendly* in a frankly too good-looking kind of way, if that was possible. He had obviously forgotten about the little incident, as she preferred to think of it, and she was immensely relieved about that.

'You should back your book up,' she advised.

'Good idea. Thank you.' In a minute she would make a bolt for it and Theo wasn't having that. Now that he had made his mind up, a calm sense of purpose had settled over him. He took a couple of steps towards her and noticed how she flinched, as nervous as a kitten. What did she imagine he was going to do? The answer was as swift in coming as it was obvious. She was wary of him touching her. He wondered what scared her more—the thought of his touch or the prospect of her response.

Without guilt yapping at his heels, Theo felt a spurt of pure adrenaline rush through him as he contemplated the sweet scent of seduction.

If someone had told him a fortnight ago that he would have been looking at another woman like this, enjoying the anticipation of bedding her, he would have floored them for daring to insult the memory of the woman he had so nearly married.

Now his eyes drifted lazily over her face, appreciating the rise of delicate colour to her cheeks.

'Am I making you nervous?' he asked.

'No! Why should you?'

'Because the last time I saw you the situation between us got a little out of hand…' He strolled towards her, hands in his pockets. 'Neither of us meant it to.' While he spoke, Theo maintained direct eye contact with her. She might be feisty, but she was also as gullible as hell and the combination was intriguing.

'I'd…really rather not talk about it…' Sophie stammered. She drew in a sharp breath and tilted her chin up.

'Well, I'd quite like to…' Theo said mildly. Now he was standing inches away from her. Yes, the door was clear but could she make a dash for it? No. Circumnavigating him would have been as straightforward as circumnavigating a mountain blindfolded and also, deliberately or not, he had thrown down a gauntlet. Discuss this, he seemed to be saying, or else risk being seen as running away.

'Why?' Sophie gulped. Her throat felt dry and she had to look away. His eyes were throwing her into a tizzy.

'Look, why don't we have some coffee? You have my word that I won't lay a finger on you... Unless, of course, you ask...'

Sophie gasped at the softly spoken, intensely sexy offer and then realised that he must be joking. Probably just to gauge her reaction. She already knew that he thought her gauche and inexperienced and mouthy with it, and he would find it funny to wind her up. Come to think of it, there was something of the predator to him and didn't predators enjoy playing with their victims before they moved in for the kill?

Sophie laughed shakily to herself at the fanciful train of thought.

But, when she met his eyes, she felt her skin begin to prickle in dreadful awareness. 'Very funny,' she managed to say in a strangled voice.

'Come on. Your nervousness is making *me* nervous.' His smile was reassuring. 'Take the coat off. Now that the heating's working it's warm enough in here to walk around in shorts and a T-shirt. I didn't think that old places could store heat that effectively.' Suddenly it was vitally important that he didn't frighten her away. This might just be his temporary salvation, just a sliver of normality unexpectedly offered to him, but he wanted it so badly it hurt.

That said, he would seduce but never force. That wasn't his style and never could be. If she was truly wary enough to keep her distance, then he would accept it.

He contemplated returning to London, the same faces at the same society dos. He wondered whether this strange release he had found here would continue to work once he returned to normal life or whether he would be plunged back into the limbo he had left behind. Here, he thought of Elena but she didn't haunt him.

He started walking away, not to the kitchen but towards the cosy sitting room, hoping she would follow. She didn't. When he looked around, she was rooted to the same spot.

'You're not coming…' Theo said with a touch of incredulity and Sophie maintained an admirably stony expression.

'Very observant.'

'Why not? I told you,' he continued, trying to fight down the edginess creeping into his voice, 'I won't bite.'

'And I told you that I don't want to discuss the inappropriate situation that took place. If you can disrespect what I say, then I'm free to ignore what you say.'

Theo stared at her and wondered how the hell he could ever have thought her gullible. Her face was red with embarrassment but, hell, that hadn't stopped her from speaking her mind.

'We have to discuss it,' he grated. She didn't budge and, red-faced or not, she looked him squarely in the face and refused to back down. Theo was beginning to feel impotent in the face of such outright female lack of co-operation.

'Why?' Sophie asked.

'Because…' he delivered his sentence with heavy-handed, thinly veiled patience '…you are my landlady. We're going to need to meet occasionally and we need to get this out in the open, talk about it so that it doesn't hang between us the way it's doing now.'

'It's only hanging between us because you brought it up,' Sophie pointed out. Going through her head was the thought that she had never been so achingly aware of a man in her life before. He oozed sex appeal and it didn't seem fair. It was bad enough having a routine conversation with him, far less a conversation to do with sex. Just bracketing those two harmless words, *Theo* and *sex*, in the same sentence was enough to make her mind do all manner of wild leap-frogging.

'It's hanging between us because it happened!'

'Yes, and I'm prepared to pretend it never did.'

Theo greeted this remark with stunned silence. In his world, at least the world he had once inhabited for years, in his carefree pre-Elena days, he had been able to play women with the finesse of a musician playing his instrument. It had always been a mutually enjoyable experience. The lazy talk of sex, dropped negligently into a conversation while his eyes expanded on the subject and promised pleasures that could only be guessed at.

'I mean,' Sophie took up the thread of her conversation, 'discussing it and having a post mortem isn't going to change anything. What we have to agree on is that nothing like that will take place again and I would appreciate it if you don't…don't…drop any innuendoes into the conversation. You might find it funny, but I don't.'

Sophie weathered the silence which stretched between them with the tautness of tightly pulled elastic. She was beginning to think that she had misheard his earlier remark and misread the situation. And why, she thought with sudden agonising clarity, had she warned him not to touch her again? As if he couldn't resist her womanly charms? No wonder he was standing there, lost for words and staring at her as though she had taken leave of her senses! Lord knew, he had probably wanted to give *her* a little speech about keeping her hands to herself!

She gathered herself together and pursed her lips. 'Right. So I only came here to tell you about the electricity going. There's a proper fireplace in the sitting room and also in the bedrooms, so if it gets very cold you are welcome to light them. I haven't ordered in a huge amount of logs as yet but there are enough stacked by the fire downstairs to tide you over until the current comes back and the heating can go on again.'

'I'm not likely to be using the bedroom in the morning, am I? So there should be no need for me to light a fire in it, and I think I'll be able to manage for a few hours without falling into a state of hypothermia.'

Theo, piqued that his attempt at seduction had fallen crushingly flat, was at pains to sound as normal as possible but he was still bemused at the unsavoury and novel sensation of being blown out of the water.

And, now that she had said what she had to say, he could tell that she was itching to be off. And he should be more than happy to see the back of her, he decided. Fate might have ironically chosen to remind him at this point in time that he was still alive and still a healthy red-blooded male, but the woman was not worth pursuit. Least of all to a man who had never had the need to pursue any woman in his life before. Not, he mused, even Elena. She may have captured his heart with her delicate China doll prettiness and her sweetly subservient nature, but their attraction had been immediate and mutual. He frowned at the bristling little figure standing in front of him.

'And how do *you* intend to while away the morning, considering all useful activity will grind to a halt while the power is off?'

'Useful activity doesn't necessarily mean work,' Sophie pointed out.

'You mean you won't be cooped up in your office sifting through paperwork?'

'Someone's got to do it! You make it sound as though I

actually enjoy sitting there, staring at piles of paper and wondering which bundle to go through first!'

'Well, what would you rather do?'

'Anything! Go for a walk on the beach! Get to see a movie for the first time in six months! Eat out at a fancy restaurant, which is something I haven't done since forever! Sorry.' She shrugged lightly, inviting him to laugh at her overblown response, but he didn't. His eyes narrowed and he stared at her in silence.

'Why are you sorry?' he asked eventually. It seemed strange to be having a conversation with the width of the hallway separating them.

Sophie, wondering how it was that she was managing to have a conversation with the man when she had been literally on the way out, took a few steps towards the door. 'Because I really should leave you to get on with your work,' she said, constrained to be polite after her outburst earlier on. 'I guess you might have to resort to longhand if you work tomorrow! Isn't that always such a shock to the system when we've all become so accustomed to computers?'

She could feel the energy pulsing out of him as she neared him and finally arrived at the safe haven of the door handle. Sophie grasped it and turned round to glance at Theo over her shoulder.

'They're usually pretty reliable at predicting the hours of the power cuts, but let me know…'

'…if I want anything. Yes, I think I've got that message by now…'

The problem was, he thought, as she vanished into the darkness, leaving him acutely aware of his very palpable frustration, the one thing he *did* want, she did not seem obliged to give him.

CHAPTER FIVE

WHEN Theo thought about Elena, he thought about everything that was delicate and feminine. The minute he had laid eyes on her, he had been drawn by her soft girlish beauty and her quiet charm. For the first time in his life his motives had been free of lust and the driving urge to get a woman into bed. Yes, he had been physically attracted to her, but bigger and more overwhelming than that attraction had been his urge to take care of her.

Elena, coming at a time in his life when he had been subconsciously thinking of settling down, had fulfilled every fantasy he had ever nurtured about the perfect woman.

She had been almost excessively pretty—blonde hair, blue eyes and none of the raunchy glamour associated with the mixture. Raunchy had always been fine for Theo when it came to women he slept with, but when it came to a prospective wife there was no way that that look was going to do. Despite his savvy, Theo had a very defined traditionalist streak. What was acceptable to wine and dine and eventually disengage from, was not acceptable when it came to sharing his life.

Elena, with her angelic good looks, had been eminently suitable wife material.

CATHY WILLIAMS   83

And she'd been deferential without being characterless. Of course, he had never been attracted to the argumentative type, but Elena had been deferential in the most charmingly attractive way. He could remember sitting across from her at the dinner table in one of those wildly expensive restaurants which he usually avoided but which seemed appropriate given his desire to impress her, could remember the way she had gazed at him with a soft smile on her lips, the way she had listened with her head cocked to one side and her eyes shining with appreciation. He had known from the very beginning that she would never criticise. She would be the soothing balm and, for Theo, that was a compelling aspect of her personality.

Throw into the mixture the fact that he would have been making a desirable match as far as both families were concerned, and the pedestal on which he had placed her became unassailable.

Theo wondered whether he would have continued mourning her disappearance from his life forever if he had remained in London. He knew now and had known for a while that he had allowed, indeed encouraged, his emotions to go into deep freeze. To start with, it had been a protective mechanism but then he had become accustomed to the freeze. In the end, it had felt good not to feel.

Lying in bed now, with a half-read business manual next to him and the prospect of a morning without the use of his computer, Theo contemplated the vagary of fate that had brought him to this pass.

He folded his hands behind his head and stared up at the ceiling.

What was it about this woman that had managed to get under his skin?

She was disagreeable and prickly a lot of the time. He doubted that she had a sweetly submissive bone in her body. Theo, used to viewing all problems in life as soluble, could not for the hell of him work out why he was bothering with a woman who rattled him when, without too much effort, he could easily find one who didn't. Considering things logically, why would he voluntarily put himself into a situation that had the potential to give him a headache? Women, he firmly believed, should never give men headaches. They were the gentle sex and their duty was to calm.

He muttered an oath under his breath, snatched up the manual and attempted to get his brain round the concepts of global business protocol.

Sophie Scott was not calming. She had also rejected his advances. Theo scowled and snapped shut the business book. The laptop computer was right there, next to him, ready and waiting for him to bring it to life, but the thought of reading through yet more urgent emails bored him.

He switched off the light and let his thoughts roam freely over selected snippets of the conversation they had had earlier, dwelling on the way she had firmly but politely warned him off making a pass at her. Obviously she had never been told that to warn a man off something was to wave a red flag under his nose. Or at least that was the way it worked with Theo.

What was the point of a challenge if you didn't rise to it? Theo always rose to a challenge. He savoured the prospect of having her, of overwhelming her prudish concerns, of releasing the fire he knew was there inside her.

He woke up the following morning with an uncomfortable sensation of coldness and realised that there was no heating in the cottage. The fact that he slept without pyjamas didn't help matters. His mind was racing, though, and the cold was almost a welcome spur to the well-spring of energy he could feel inside him. He had a very quick and very cold shower and by nine-thirty he was on the way to her office.

Sitting on the floor and wrapped up in various layers of thick clothing because there was no way that Sophie was going to sit around in her coat, she was barely aware of Theo pushing open the office door.

In fact, she was not at all aware of his presence until he was looming over her; then his shadow alerted her to the fact that she was no longer alone.

With a little yelp of shock, she stumbled to her feet, sending various sheets of paper shooting off her lap on to the ground.

'What are you doing here?' she demanded, dusting herself down and glaring at him.

'Where's the rest of your motley crew?'

'You haven't answered my question.' She had pretty much given up trying to remember that she was his landlady and obliged to display good manners, even though she might not feel like it. She had been sitting on that wretched floor for the best part of an hour, simply because it had seemed easier to get down to the level of the boxes rather than continually drag them up to her level. Her jeans were dusty, her hands were dusty, her hair was probably dusty too and her clothes were a shambolic assortment of things that should really have been binned years ago but had somehow managed to slip through the net. She felt a mess and she looked a mess and there he stood, outrageously sexy in a pair of cords, a thick cream sweater and a battered leather jacket that screamed casual style.

'I thought I would drop in, maybe give you a hand with

some of this paperwork, seeing that I can't do any work myself because of the power cut.'

'You can still write without a computer,' Sophie felt constrained to point out. She hoped that it wasn't part of his game plan to spend the morning under her feet just because his computer was out of action for a few hours. 'I mean, aren't you writers supposed to be inventive?'

'I think you're thinking of people like your father.'

'I said *inventive* not *inventors*.'

'Show me what you've done already and how your filing system works.'

'You don't have to sit and help me with this.'

'In other words, you'd rather I didn't.'

'I'd work a lot faster if I don't have to stop to explain stuff to you.'

'I'm a very quick learner. You would be surprised.'

'You should use this opportunity to see something around here,' Sophie suggested desperately. 'I mean, if you really think that you can't write a chapter or two of your book without a computer.'

'Why don't you just accept my offer of help in the manner in which it was intended?' Theo said with mounting impatience. 'Especially as there is no one around at the moment to help out anyway. Where is the gang of three? Christmas shopping?'

Sophie guiltily thought of Robert. True to his word, he had not shown up but she had spent the morning half expecting him to telephone her and was relieved that he hadn't. His proposal, coming out of nowhere as it had, had shaken her to the core. He had been a friend and a helping hand to her when she had needed one but was that any reason to consider developing a relationship with him? On the other hand, she wasn't getting any younger and they *did* get along, at least on

CATHY WILLIAMS   87

a superficial level, which was the only level they had previously enjoyed.

What was the harm in just seeing whether there was something there that could be developed further?

'Don't tell me the boyfriend has deserted the sinking ship?' Theo slid open the drawer of one of the metal filing cabinets and began looking at the files.

'You need a computer,' he said, as the level of paperwork became ever clearer. 'It's the only way you'll be able to keep track of everything here and, aside from that, it's a bloody fire hazard.'

'I've got a computer,' Sophie told him airily.

'Where is it?'

'Upstairs. I just haven't got around to…logging some of this stuff in… It takes time, you know… All that computer work, et cetera… I mean, it's all right for you. You just have to sit there telling stories and typing away.'

It occurred to Theo that the whole figment of his occupation was becoming a burden, but he quickly reminded himself how much more satisfying it was to be incognito, at least for a short while. Hadn't he lived his entire life with the weight of expectation on his shoulders? Without any siblings to share the responsibility, he had had little option but to fulfil his duty as son and heir to a shipping empire. Just as well he had found it to his liking. All the same, it was good to be suddenly in this make-believe role, with only himself to please and absolutely no one else.

'I know a thing or two about computers. I could have a look at what you've done so far, see whether it mightn't require some updating.'

'You know about computers? How do you know about computers? No! Let me guess! The way you seem to know about *everything*. Information just wafts into you, through osmosis! Lucky you.'

'You haven't logged any of this on to a computer, have you?'

Sophie wanted to ask him how he had the nerve to waltz into her office and begin making assumptions about her approach to the workload. Did he think that it was a walk in the park trying to come to terms with your father's death and sort out the chaos he had left behind without you ever suspecting a thing at the same time? However, there he was, sitting there and looking as though he knew what he was doing, which, of course, he didn't, and she just wanted to dump the lot on to him and ask him to deal with it while she went to her bed and slept for a few weeks till it was all cleared up.

'I've been meaning to...' Sophie admitted sulkily and Theo tut-tutted under his breath.

'Well, we can't do anything at the moment but, as soon as the power is back, I suggest we install a simple program so that we can collate all the information scattered in these boxes.'

'We...?' Sophie felt obliged to reveal the extent of her ignorance of all things technical. 'Computers and I have never had much of a friendship.'

'That being the case, I'm surprised what's-his-name couldn't have helped you out there.'

'I think we were just so busy trying to get the stuff together that...that...'

'That it never occurred to you that there might be a far quicker way to do it...?' He grabbed a stack of files and strolled over to her desk, where he proceeded to drag the nearest chair to hers so that he could position himself next to her. 'Okay. Look at these.' He pointed to some symbols and picked out various key words, which meant frankly nothing to Sophie's untrained eyes. 'We could install a program that would automatically collate information that belongs under the same banner. So, for example, experiments based on certain solutions, where your father was in contact with the same person at roughly the same time, could automatically reach the same file at the click of a button.'

'You could do that?' Sophie asked, seriously impressed. She desperately wished that she had paid a bit more attention in IT at school. 'How?' she demanded. 'Did you do a computer course at college?'

Computer course? *College?*

'I dabbled in it at university,' Theo conceded.

'Oh, right.'

'Surprised?' He leaned forward and rested his elbows on his thighs.

'Oh, no. Not at all. Well, not that you went to university…I'm just surprised that you took an interest in something like computing. Was it part of your creative writing course?'

'Whoever said anything about creative writing?' That little white lie by Gloria, delivered for all the right reasons, to protect him because as a high profile name in business he might have attracted unwanted attention, was now beginning to haunt Theo. He refused to enlarge upon it by fabricating a mystery past.

Sophie frowned. 'Well, what did you do at university?' she asked.

'Economics and law.'

'You're kidding, right?'

'Why should I be kidding?' Theo asked dryly.

'Because…' Sophie spluttered, predicting that this would lead right back to his conviction that she had stereotyped him. 'So…yes, I can see that you might be interested in computers if you liked law and economics…'

Theo grinned. 'Does that make me a boring person, do you think?'

'You're the least boring person I've ever met!' The words were out before Sophie had a chance to think about how they sounded. She cringed back, mortified, into the chair and tried to think how she could explain that what she *had meant* was that he was too arrogant, too opinionated and too clever by half to ever be considered *boring*. Which didn't mean that he was fun or exciting or stimulating!

'Is that a fact?' Theo drawled lazily.

'I *mean…*' *What did she mean?* He was looking at her expectantly, waiting for her answer. Didn't he realise that that was just plain conceited—to enjoy hearing himself discussed?

'My computer isn't very up-to-date,' Sophie said, changing the subject. 'I couldn't afford to buy a new one when I started my teacher training course and I only realised afterwards that there's a reason why people get rid of their computers after a couple of years. They just become obsolete. So I hope this amazing program you have in mind won't be too much for it to handle.'

Theo leaned back in his chair and looked at her. Just when he felt as though he was close to working her out, she skittered away and he was left trying to figure out her complexities. She didn't find him boring—she had just said so even though he had had the sneaking suspicion that she might have wished she hadn't. She was attracted to him, although she was determined not to act upon it. He wondered whether there was something going on with the Robert character, although she had been at pains to deny it. Where was the man, anyway? She hadn't actually answered his question when he had asked earlier.

'I'll check and see,' Theo said indifferently. 'We could always get a new one.'

'*Get a new one?*' Sophie looked at him as though he had taken leave of his senses.

'Computers have come down in price substantially over the years…'

'And getting one would still cost too much, never mind how substantially they've come down in price over the years! Why do you think I've had to rent out the cottage? I need the money!' She cast a despairing look around her. 'I've only been through half of this. There's more stuff upstairs and more yet in the cottage, buried in boxes in the attic. And I've unearthed more bills than I can shake a stick at. You have no idea! Your rent has already been eaten up paying off creditors. So when it comes to flinging another few hundred pounds in the direction of a new computer, then you can think again.'

The sympathy on his face was too much. Sophie stood up, stretched and tried to gather herself by walking over to the kettle to make a cup of coffee for them. Belatedly she remembered that no power meant no functioning kettle, and she turned to look at him with an apologetic smile.

'Sorry. You haven't come here to take time out so that you can be bored by my problems.'

'Is there no one who can guarantee you a loan until such time as you can pay them back?'

Sophie thought of Robert and hesitated. 'Not really…'

'What does *not really* mean?'

'Robert *has* said that he would be willing to bail me out. I mean, obviously that would depend on how much I end up owing…'

'Where is he now?' Theo frowned in frank dismissal. 'Anyway, tell me, what's the catch?'

'Oh, no catch!' Sophie waved a little too airily. 'I'd make you some coffee but no electricity for the kettle. Are you all right with the heating off? It's just a localised power cut. A few miles down the road and you can easily do some shopping, find somewhere warm to sit and have some tea…'

Theo wondered why she was suddenly so desperate to change the subject. 'There's no such thing as a free lunch, Sophie, and I can tell from the look on your face that whatever offer your friend came up with has some strings attached to it. So what are they? Hefty interest rate? The cottage as collateral? I'd be very careful about taking money from a loan shark.' He felt himself getting hot under the collar at the thought of an opportunist taking her for every penny she had. And he would because Sophie, for all those forthright mannerisms that would send any normal man's blood pressure soaring in irritation, was an innocent in the world of finance. It would have been no problem for him to give her the money but he knew that she would never accept it, not even if she knew the full extent of his massive personal fortune.

'Robert's no loan shark! Anyway, either he's dull and insecure or he's a clever opportunist. He can't be both!' Sophie objected hotly, already regretting her slip-up.

'I never said dull… *You* just did. Interesting. Well, what repayment scheme does he have in mind?' Theo asked, raising his eyebrows in a mixture of curiosity and cynicism.

'Stop twisting my words. All I'm saying is that I've been offered a life belt if I think I need one. And if I mentioned the word *dull* it's because that's the picture you insist on conjuring up every time his name is mentioned! Never mind that you've met him for five seconds!'

She was waffling, he noticed, without actually enlightening him, which sharpened his curiosity still further.

'Well?' he pressed. 'I'm very experienced in all matters

relating to money so I'm immune to surprises in that particular quarter.'

'You do blow your own trumpet, don't you?' Sophie said tartly. 'Is there any area you would admit to *not* being good at?'

Writing, Theo considered, except of the most prosaic kind. 'I've been clever at picking things up along the way.' He spread his hands expansively, with an expression of *don't blame me if I'm good at everything*.

That, of course, was what did it. Sophie, never one to see the benefit of taking someone down a few notches just to watch the expression on their face, could not resist the temptation to wipe that smirk off Theo's face. The devil inside her made her nod in a knowing way, totally understanding the hideous disadvantages of just being brilliant at everything, with the possible exception of mending central heating devices in old cottages. Yes, being that sharp *would* make him immune to surprises.

'Well, I'll confess what the catch is, although I don't think anyone would really call it a catch. As such.' She paused for a few dramatic seconds. 'Robert has proposed to me.'

'Proposed what?'

'Proposed that we get married!' Sophie said through gritted teeth. Was the possibility of someone asking for her hand in marriage such a difficult concept to take on board?

'You're joking!'

'No. No, I am *not* joking. You might think you know *everything* because you're *so clever at picking things up along the way*, but you obviously don't know women that well or you would know that they *never* joke about marriage proposals.'

For some reason, Theo was finding it hard to take in what Sophie had just said. Why, he had no idea. When he approached her revelation logically, he could see that, as solutions went, it didn't get better. A man wanting to help his woman out of her financial mess because he loved her.

So what if he had been temporarily attracted to the woman? He almost laughed aloud at his crazy overreaction to her news! As if there weren't a million other fish in the sea! True, he had imagined that the strangeness of his circumstances had been responsible for opening up a chink in his protective armour, but really, thinking about it, that wasn't the case at all. The change of scenery had been a catalyst. He would never forget Elena—indeed there would never be another woman to match her—but his body was responding once again. It was a bitter truth he would have to swallow. He was still a man with needs that had to be met.

But this woman was not an integral part of that. He had thought that returning to London, getting back to his daily reality, would return him to the brooding workaholic that he had previously been, seeking out dangerous pursuits in an attempt to distract himself from his private pain. Now he considered the possibility of his life returning to some level of normality.

'And…?' he prompted. 'Did you accept his kind offer? I suppose it would have been too much temptation to resist.'

Sophie hesitated, already regretting the impulse that had seen her confess something that should have been a private matter. 'I'm thinking about it,' she mumbled.

'I had no idea your relationship with the man was so serious.'

Nor did I, Sophie thought, wondering how she could entice him away from the topic.

'And all he wants is your hand in marriage?' Theo quizzed, his brows knitted in a frown.

'Amazing, isn't it?'

Theo focused on Sophie's face and registered the smug

expression—just the sort of smug expression that could well and truly get under a man's skin and try his patience to the limits.

'Not really, when you think about it. As I said, an insecure kind of boy—your plight is probably the one thing guaranteed to make him feel like a man…' Okay, so it was an arrogant, incendiary statement, but for some reason Theo was finding it distasteful to think of Sophie and that wet rag having any kind of relationship.

'Thanks for the compliment!'

'Probably one of those men who can't wait for the whole family deal… Well, it sure beats the hell out of playing a field they don't feel very comfortable in…'

'Oh, and that's what every woman fights shy of——a family man! Because we *all* want a rampant womaniser!'

'I *am* usually right when it comes to reading people.' Theo shrugged.

'Oh, right. Yet another one of those handy talents you picked up along the way.'

'Very handy,' Theo agreed readily, enjoying the way she bristled as he ignored the sarcasm. 'Life's a lot easier if you can read people accurately and the way I read it is that his proposal might have set you thinking, but is it enough to overcome the fact that you don't actually love the man? Because if you loved the guy you certainly wouldn't tolerate me describing him as a wimp…'

'Your opinion doesn't matter to me, actually. And what's love anyway?' she scoffed. She had been encouraged to think that it was tumultuous and wonderful. Her parents had had one of those passionate, enduring romances and had misinformed her that she, too, would one day have the same. Well, as far as Sophie was concerned, she was still waiting. So far, she hadn't even had a broken heart. No one had come close to being that meaningful a presence in her life. Which, she told herself, was obviously good. Who wanted a broken heart? On top of everything else at the moment, that would be absolutely the last straw.

And if there was no love, then why not see marriage as a business arrangement? Robert was proposing a business arrangement. He said that he was attracted to her, which she found extraordinary given the success with which he had managed to camouflage his feelings. She didn't think he loved her, but he liked her well enough and was it so odd that he would see the whole business of marriage from the same jaded viewpoint as she did?

'If love was that special, then how come the divorce rate is so high?'

Theo didn't say anything. 'Is this your way of talking yourself into marrying someone you don't care about?'

'This is my way of answering your question,' Sophie muttered. 'Anyway, if you're such a fan of the whole Love thing, how come you're not married?' She would have bet her house that he felt the same way as she was stridently pretending to. He just *looked* too worldly wise to have a romantic bone in his body.

'Oh, you have a point,' Theo said coolly. 'Why don't you show me where your computer is and I can start working on this program as soon as power is restored?'

'Oh.' Sophie felt a very brief jarring sensation of disappointment at the abrupt change in conversation; then she was hastening to assure him that there was no need for him to involve himself in her situation. In fact, she hurried on to add, she would really rather he didn't.

'Why? It would make life a lot easier for you and would

The Harlequin Reader Service® — Here's how it works:

Accepting your 2 free books and 2 free mystery gifts places you under no obligation to buy anything. You may keep the books and gifts and return the shipping statement marked "cancel." If you do not cancel, about a month later we'll send you 6 additional books and bill you just $3.80 each in the U.S., or $4.47 each in Canada, plus 25¢ shipping & handling per book and applicable taxes if any.* That's the complete price and — compared to cover prices of $4.50 each in the U.S. and $5.25 each in Canada — it's quite a bargain! You may cancel at any time, but if you choose to continue, every month we'll send you 6 more books, which you may either purchase at the discount price or return to us and cancel your subscription.

*Terms and prices subject to change without notice. Sales tax applicable in N.Y. Canadian residents will be charged applicable provincial taxes and GST. All orders subject to approval. Credit or debit balances in a customer's account(s) may be offset by any other outstanding balance owed by or to the customer. Please allow 4 to 6 weeks for delivery.

If offer card is missing write to: Harlequin Reader Service, 3010 Walden Ave., P.O. Box 1867, Buffalo NY 14240-1867

NO POSTAGE
NECESSARY
IF MAILED
IN THE
UNITED STATES

BUSINESS REPLY MAIL
FIRST-CLASS MAIL   PERMIT NO. 717-003   BUFFALO, NY

POSTAGE WILL BE PAID BY ADDRESSEE

HARLEQUIN READER SERVICE
3010 WALDEN AVE
PO BOX 1867
BUFFALO NY 14240-9952

GET FREE BOOKS and FREE GIFTS WHEN YOU PLAY THE...

Lucky 7

SLOT MACHINE GAME!

Just scratch off the silver box with a coin. Then check below to see the gifts you get!

YES!

I have scratched off the silver box. Please send me the 2 free Harlequin Presents® books and 2 free gifts for which I qualify. I understand I am under no obligation to purchase any books, as explained on the back of this card.

306 HDL EF37   **106 HDL EF4Y**

FIRST NAME	LAST NAME

ADDRESS

APT.#	CITY

STATE/PROV.	ZIP/POSTAL CODE

7	7	7	**Worth TWO FREE BOOKS plus 2 BONUS Mystery Gifts!**
🍒	🍒	🍒	**Worth TWO FREE BOOKS!**
♣	♣	♣	**Worth ONE FREE BOOK!**
🔔	🔔	🍒	**TRY AGAIN!**

www.eHarlequin.com

(H-P-12/06)

also be a far more efficient method of keeping track of all these documents.'

'I wouldn't be able to pay you for it…'

For some reason, that objection made Theo savagely angry. 'I don't believe I asked for payment,' he said coldly.

'I wouldn't feel happy about you taking time out from your writing to help me.' Sophie's chin went up. 'I'm not a charity case.'

'No, but you're a fool.'

'I beg your pardon!'

'Why look a gift horse in the mouth?' Theo said harshly. 'I'm offering to lend you a hand. Take the offer with good grace.'

'As you said, though, there's no such thing as a free lunch. What will your price be?'

Theo's eyes narrowed on her until Sophie was squirming in her chair. Wrong question, she belatedly realised, but yet again the words had popped out of her mouth before she could sift them over in her head.

'Consider it a trade-off. Your cottage has done wonders for…my writer's block, as it happens and one good turn deserves another.' But he had a sudden image of her paying him back with her body, lying beneath him, writhing with passion, her eyes languorous and heavy with desire.

Not to be. He had always made a point of zero involvement with a woman who was tied up with another man.

'Where will you…do it?'

Theo looked at her, disoriented for a few seconds by the very graphic nature of the image in his head. 'Where will I do…what?'

'The program,' Sophie explained patiently. 'You're welcome to work here with us, but it's very cramped compared to the cottage. But no problem, of course, if you'd prefer here…I mean, the files are all around…' Literally. Which in no way could be construed as an advantage as far as she could see. She tried to picture him sitting here in the office with them for hours on end, or however long it took him to install the program, and her stomach did a funny little dip that left her breathless.

'No. I'll take it to the cottage with me. Are there any files on it you'd rather I didn't see?'

'Like what?'

'Use your imagination,' Theo said dryly.

'No. No! Just work stuff.'

'Right. Well, no time like the present.' He stood up and so did Sophie. The way to the upstairs flat was through the back, and she could feel the hairs on the back of her neck standing up on end as he followed closely behind her.

The flat was small and functional. It contained all the basic requirements to make life palatable, though only for brief periods of time. At the end of the narrow corridor was a kitchen which was really only good for essential cooking and tea and coffee and off the corridor was a bedroom, a bathroom and a spare room which her father had used for his office and which she used for her desk-cum-dressing table.

The computer was on the desk. In his head, Theo had assumed it would be a laptop computer. It wasn't. It was as big as a television set and, with his recovering foot, he would be unable to carry it.

'I didn't think,' Sophie said quietly and he spun round to look at her. 'Your foot. This is going to be way too heavy for you to carry.' She saw a flash of fierce pride in his eyes and felt a moment of real empathy for him. 'How did it happen?' she asked curiously.

Theo shrugged and sat down. He tapped his finger idly on

the mouse mat, frustrated that a simple task, that he would have thought nothing of once, was now beyond his reach.

'By me being an idiot,' Theo told her roughly. She had pulled up a chair and was sitting by him, probably on the verge of pouring some good old-fashioned Christian sympathy all over him. He didn't want it and he didn't need it. He felt the inadequacy of his body like a shameful physical blow. 'I thought I could master a black run and it turned out that nature had a little lesson in store for me. And now,' he scorned, 'I suppose I must expect your pity. Spare me. Please.'

'I don't think it's possible for anyone to *pity* you, Theo,' she said truthfully. 'You're too…*dominant*.' She gave him a crooked smile.

'Is that a good thing, I wonder…' Theo murmured.

'It has its…advantages…' Sophie answered. 'Ordering drinks at a crowded bar…getting rid of pesky door-to-door salesmen…showing a yapping dog who's boss…'

Theo smiled and the blast of it nearly took her breath away. In fact, she was sure that her breathing stopped, just for a few seconds. Her heart rate also seemed to have slowed.

'Useful, then.'

'Useful, yes.'

'But not particularly attractive…'

Sophie, mesmerised, could only stare at the harsh angular beauty of his face, softened by the slight smile playing on his lips. She was barely aware of leaning forward, of her eyes half closing or of the sigh that escaped before she kissed him.

CHAPTER SIX

WITHIN that kiss lay the essence of forbidden passion. It was strong and urgent and shamefully hungry.

Theo's surprise lasted all of two seconds, then he savoured the sweetness of her mouth and the soft yielding of her body inclined towards his. He hadn't moved. Instead, Sophie had half risen from her chair so that she could lean into him and she moaned softly as he placed his hand on her naked waist, where her jumper had risen up.

'I'm sorry...' She drew back for air, confused and disoriented by the impulse that had overwhelmed her.

'For what?' Theo had his hand curled into her hair and, instead of removing it, he pulled her towards him and kissed her along her jawline, which sent hot and cold flushes racing through her body. He had planned to back away from her. She was involved with another man and he was no poacher, but her kiss had put paid to any such noble intentions. Wasn't all fair in love and war? And she couldn't be that involved with Robert if she was willing to fling herself at another man. Theo, starved of physical contact for so long, felt himself taking deep breaths to keep his body in some kind of check.

'This shouldn't have happened.' Appalled by her own behaviour, Sophie tried to wriggle back but the hand behind her was like steel. The more she wriggled, the more firmly it remained in place. Eventually, she abandoned the unequal struggle. 'I'm not comfortable talking to you like this. I'm going to pull a muscle in my back in a minute.'

'So I let you go and you run away. Then, when we next meet, you tell me that we should pretend that nothing happened.' He slipped his hand under the jumper and ran his finger along her spine until she thought she might just pass out from the sensation. 'You don't have to run away,' he murmured, 'and it's no good pretending that there's nothing between us...'

'There *is* nothing...between us...! And could you please stop doing that...?'

'Doing what?' Theo allowed his finger to travel the dangerous route down her spine until he found the gap in the waistband of her trousers, just big enough for his gently exploring finger to linger along the stretchy Lycra band of her underwear. 'Turning you on?'

Sophie shivered and made one last desperate attempt to make contact with Planet Earth. 'You mustn't...we mustn't... It's just not...*right*...'

'Why? Because there's a man in your life?'

Sophie, who hadn't given Robert a moment's thought, mumbled something that was totally inaudible. Her head was telling her to use any excuse at hand to prise herself out of this compromising position, but her body was singing a different tune, a wickedly seductive tune. Torn between conflicting demands, she could only listen to the velvety purr of his voice and knew, with horror, that she *wanted* to be persuaded because her body was screaming out to be touched and not just here and there, but everywhere.

'You're not serious about him, Sophie,' Theo murmured softly. 'Come and sit on my lap and I'll tell you why...'

Sophie had never sat on a man's lap before. Well, she guessed, she would have sat on her dad's when she was a toddler, but never in a situation like this, when the atmosphere was thick with unspoken needs and the innocent act of sitting on his lap took on a whole new meaning.

But, of course, it was still within her grasp to pull away whenever she wanted. That was the thought that feebly ran through her head as she edged towards him and was spared a final decision because he yanked her down, forcing her to hold on to him to save herself from an undignified landing.

'There. Now, isn't that better? Warmer too, with the heating off. It's a known fact that the best way to keep warm is through close proximity to another body. You would be surprised the amount of heat we give off.'

Sophie made a strangled noise and then lost herself in his indecently sexy eyes—the purest and deepest of greens, fringed by lashes that were thick and dark and ridiculously long for a man. She felt her body melt a little and the hands around his neck imperceptibly moved upwards so that she could feel the texture of his black hair.

'So…I was saying…' He rested the flat of his hand on her thigh and gently massaged through the denim of her jeans. 'The boy—Robert—he may have proposed and perhaps, just perhaps, he's deluded himself into thinking that the two of you would be good for one another, but you know and I know that that wouldn't be the case, would it?'

Sophie hoped that he wasn't expecting an answer to that because she was incapable of doing anything near as coherent as that at the moment, when his hand was managing to send urgent messages to her brain that told her to open her legs just slightly, enough for him to move upwards, while his eyes remained pinned to her face.

'I mean…' Theo mused softly, taking his time because his body wanted to race ahead and just take what it had missed for so long. 'That man's no good for you, whatever story he spins about being your knight in shining armour.'

'Every girl needs a knight in shining armour…' The observation ended on a gasp as his questing hand found the zip of her jeans and tugged it down, exposing her sensible black cotton underwear. Still talking in that lazy silky voice, Theo slipped his hand under her pants and he groaned when she arched back, eyes closed, enjoying his fingers as they played with her.

'I think we should go somewhere where there's a bed,' he said.

Through the blurred mist of her thoughts, Sophie knew that this was her last chance to pull away. At this point, she could use any excuse she wanted. They would both know the truth of the situation and there was no excuse that wouldn't reek of hypocritical emptiness.

Sophie had never been a risk-taker. She had never rebelled during her teenage years. Her minor disobediences had been along the lines of feigning illness to skip a test or refusing to carry on with piano lessons even though her parents wanted her to continue. She had been a goody two shoes, content to watch from the sidelines while other girls broke the rules.

Going with Theo would constitute the biggest risk she could take.

'Let's go,' she heard herself say, peppering his mouth with kisses.

Two words and she metaphorically jumped off the side of the cliff. It wasn't just that she was going to sleep with him. No. Deep inside her she knew that it was much more than that. She was going to sleep with a man she barely knew, someone to whom she responded, often antagonistically, on a gut level.

There had been no courtship, no dating, no romance and it was a situation that was going nowhere. She was willingly going to go against everything she had always believed in and she was looking forward to it!

That realisation made her walk just that bit more provocatively as they headed to the bedroom. With each step, she could feel her excitement increasing until they were finally in the bedroom and the double bed was staring them in the face, screaming an invitation.

Sophie, released from a lifetime of conformity, moved towards the window and drew the curtains, shutting out the weak, intrusive winter sunlight. When she turned round, it was to find Theo standing by the door, looking at her.

'It's basic.'

'It's perfect,' Theo told her roughly. When she began to hitch her jumper over her head, he stopped her and began walking towards her.

'Body heat. Remember?'

'Meaning…what?' It was madness, but for a one-night stand, or rather a one-morning stand that was going nowhere, he was making her feel incredibly sexy and very, very wanton.

'Meaning we should get naked…when we're in very close proximity to one another…'

He placed his hands in the hollow of her back and ground her against him so that there was no escaping the reality of his erection and, when she felt as if she was going to faint from what it was doing to her, he began kissing her—long, sweet kisses that left her breathless and weak.

The soft willingness of her body was, for Theo, like a life raft to a drowning man. Had he realised how much he had missed this most basic of human contact? After Elena, he had willed himself to feel nothing and so he had felt nothing. Not a twinge of sexual awareness in the presence of a woman, no matter how beautiful or physically desirable or even available the woman in question had been.

And, even when he had been with Elena, sex had not been on the menu. Her ultra-feminine fragility had not encouraged the more rampantly male side of him and Theo had been content to wait until such time as she dictated.

It had been a very long time since his body had been satisfied. Theo buried his face in her Sophie's fair, silky hair and breathed in that beautiful fragrance, a mixture of shampoo and hair conditioner, that always struck him as essentially female.

And, miraculously, he felt no sense of betrayal. On no front did this woman constitute a threat to his precious memories. She was a safety valve. He heard her moan softly as he pressed her still harder against him.

'I'd carry you to the bed myself, but…'

'But you'd like to spare me the embarrassment of being responsible for you ending up in hospital with a broken back…?'

Theo laughed. She had a sense of humour, which was good. It meant she wasn't making this into a big deal.

'I think, in a case like that, we'd *both* be embarrassed.' But, actually, he really would have liked to have carried her over to the bed and very gently deposited her on it. It was an amusing notion considering he thought himself the least romantic man on the face of the earth.

But one thing he wouldn't let her do was take her clothes off. *That* was something he intended to do himself so that he could savour every second of the experience very slowly.

Sophie found herself luxuriating in the experience, feeling like the cat that had suddenly and unexpectedly landed the jug of cream. In that part of her brain which was still operating—

just—she puzzled over the enigma of how she could enjoy, with such perfect blissful abandonment, the touch and feel and scent of a man who was also capable of rousing her to real anger and frustration. Like one of those nasty maths problems she could never work out for exams, Sophie dismissed the niggle and sighed as Theo began tugging down her jeans.

The drawn curtains had managed to block out most of the light but it was still far from dark in the room. Sophie watched, fascinated and turned on, the ripple of muscle along his arms and shoulders as he discarded her jeans and, kneeling at the bottom of the bed, removed his jumper. His body was as lean and as honed as any finely tuned athlete and bronzed—as perfect a male specimen as she had ever set eyes on. It briefly crossed her mind that she was taking on way more than she could handle but, like the insoluble maths problem, she shoved aside the worry.

More pressing was the thought that her underwear was simply not up to scratch. She was pretty sure that the women he had slept with, and Lord knew how many of them there had been in his life, would have worn sexy, lacy underwear. Expensive exquisite silk as opposed to bargain buy cotton.

But that little anxiety lasted all of three seconds and then there were no more thoughts as he pulled down the functional briefs and positioned himself squarely between her thighs.

It was almost painful for Theo not to give in to the overpowering urge to just take her. No more preliminaries, no more foreplay, just desperately needed gratification of his senses, but even though his body was so keyed up that a single touch and he would explode, he still wanted to satisfy her and to feel every inch of her respond to him.

He breathed in deeply to steady himself and then leant over

her and began inching her jumper upwards. He must have fantasised about this even without realising it. What else would account for the fact that he could hardly breathe as more smooth skin was revealed to his greedy gaze?

And no bra. His hands itched to touch but when he finally touched he knew that he wanted it to be with his mouth. He wanted all his senses to be satisfied.

He heard her whimper as finally the jumper was off. For a fairly slight woman, her breasts were surprisingly lush, with big well defined nipples that Theo reached forward and touched, first with his thumbs until the peaks were rock-hard and then with his tongue, his mouth, his teeth, enjoying the way she bucked against him.

He couldn't get enough of that sweet taste, pulling the nipples into his mouth and suckling on them until she whimpered that he had to stop, that she wanted him in her.

'Not yet,' Theo said, moving down, trailing his mouth along the flat planes of her stomach, circling her belly button with his tongue. He must be a glutton for punishment, he thought, not to take her at her word and release them both from the sweet torment of their needy bodies, but he was still intent on tasting every inch of her luscious body, knowing that she would respond.

He breathed in her unique smell, filling his nostrils with it, and then gently parted the folds of her womanhood. With his free hand on her stomach, he was aware of her sharp intake of breath and the jagged release of it as his tongue found the protruding sensitive bud of her femininity.

He wouldn't stay there too long. He knew that she was on the brink. Frankly, so was he. When she began to toss under his exploring tongue, Theo rose up and, with a few sharp thrusts, penetrated her.

He reared up and took them both over the edge and release was glorious, spectacular.

Their bodies were slick with perspiration when he finally lay down next to her.

He wanted to ask her what she was thinking and realised, uncomfortably, that that was just the sort of question women used to ask *him*, a question which he had always found intensely irritating because his thoughts were not meant for sharing idly after sex. Or at any time, for that matter.

He pulled her so that she was facing him and gently stroked her hair away from her face.

'Should we have done…what we just did?' Sophie breathed. She could feel anxiety buzzing around inside her. No, she did not regret abandoning her principles, but, like all principled people, she couldn't help wondering what happened next in the scenario, where was the logical progression that would make sense of her behaviour. She half hoped that he would tell her that it had all been a crashing mistake because that way she could rebuild her fortress and get back to some healthy dislike.

Instead, he gave her a lopsided grin and raised his eyebrows. 'What kind of question is that?' He kissed the corner of her mouth, which in itself provided her with the answer she was looking for. Yes…no mistake had been made. Making love with him had felt *right*.

'Are you afraid that as your lover I might start asking you to knock something off my rent?' He kissed her a little bit harder and was ridiculously gratified when she responded.

'Are *you* afraid that as my lover I might start asking *you* to pay a bit more towards the rent?'

'I would, you know…'

'Would what? I was joking.'

'Would pay more—enough to bail you out of your financial mess, in other words.'

Sophie stiffened. 'I would never, never ask you to do that.'

'I know you wouldn't. I'm offering.'

'Thanks but no thanks.' She began pulling away but he kept his hands firmly clamped on her shoulders, preventing her from going anywhere.

'I don't intend to open up an argument over this, Sophie,' Theo grated. 'It was an offer. You rejected it. That's fine. I won't broach the subject again.' He was tempted to draw her attention to that fine line between pride and stupidity but it wouldn't have gone down well, even though it enraged him to think that she would consider Robert—nondescript background Robert—as someone she might turn to in her hour of need. Still. Her life and her prerogative to run it as she saw fit. It wasn't his concern at the end of the day.

'I'm not a charity case.' Sophie was not mollified by his retreat. There could be no power play between them and no suggestion that he might rescue her from her debts. Whatever they had had to be free from all constraints, free, in a way, from the ugliness of reality—something passing to be enjoyed. It might be that their enjoyment lasted only this one time or maybe once more, but it couldn't be marred by the grinding nuts and bolts of everyday life. And talk of lending her money was everyday life at its worst.

'I don't think it's a good idea for you to help me with this computer program of yours.' Well, was lending money any different from lending time and energy? She would still feel indebted in some way and indebtedness would be the clarion call for guilt to set in. Guilt that she was doing something she shouldn't be doing, guilt that she was being used, guilt that she shouldn't be enjoying herself, not when her beloved father had died and there were so many problems to be dealt with in the wake of his death.

Theo felt that he could read this woman's mind like a book. Or maybe her face was just so transparent that her thoughts flitted across it without the benefit of concealment. He was momentarily enchanted by the concept of someone so inept at hiding what they were feeling. 'If you say so,' he murmured, taking a gamble on her response. She might not behave in a predictable fashion, but he knew enough about women to realise that certain things were predictable, and having her self-righteous tirade chopped off before it had a chance to begin would, he reckoned, be too much for her to handle.

'Well, I do. As a matter of fact.'

'Okay.'

Sophie frowned and smoothed her ruffled feathers by telling herself that at least they weren't going to have an argument because he refused to listen to her. She didn't want to argue with him. She wanted to enjoy him. It was perverse and made no sense but she wasn't going to question it. She had jumped off the side of the cliff and was free-falling, but in a wonderful way, and she wasn't going to alter its brief course.

'Good,' she told him firmly. She pressed herself against him, loving the feel of his hard masculine body against her soft feminine one. And she obviously wasn't the only one with a responsive body. She reached down and circled his arousal with her hand and gently massaged it, then she pressed it against her own moist arousal and moaned softly as his eyes darkened and his breathing became jerky.

Theo, not foreseeing the end of the conversation just yet and pretty convinced that he could swing her round to accepting his help if not his money, found himself unable to do anything but respond to what his body was doing. Although he made love with the finesse of a master, there had always been a part of him that could stand outside what was happening and remain detached, some little part of his brain that could take control of the proceedings at any given moment should the need arise. The same part of his brain which should easily have been able to resist her exploring hand and terminate the conversation when it had reached a satisfactory conclusion for him. Not so now. He was powerless to do anything but touch and feel as the motion of her hand got quicker until he felt himself on the verge of doing the unthinkable and ejaculating like a teenager unable to control himself.

He grasped her hand and groaned.

'You witch.' He laughed softly and spun her so that she was on top of him. 'Like it like this?' He pulled her face towards his and kissed her and, while he kissed her, she manoeuvred herself so that he was deep inside her, filling her with such intense pleasure that she felt breathless.

She moved on him and arched her body up so that her breasts dangled provocatively in his face, their ripe nipples teasing his mouth until he found one and sucked hard on it as she increased her tempo.

Sophie had never done anything like this before. Her sexual experiences were severely limited and she had certainly never been roused to levels of such utter abandonment. She looked down at him, at his fiercely handsome face, and shuddered as she watched him suckle on her.

Their bodies were slick with perspiration and the aroma of sex filled the air like musky sweet incense. Sophie barely noticed the sound of the central heating firing up as power was restored. She was lost, every part of her absorbed with the sensations her body was experiencing.

Their climax left her spent and oddly emotional. She sagged on top of him before rolling off but, when she went to draw the covers over her ravished body, he stilled her hand.

'No way. I want to lie here and look at you naked.' He reached out and gently feathered a touch across her breast, circling her nipple, which was still darkened from the attentions paid to it.

And, he thought, he wanted to establish that all questions about Robert had been answered. For her own sake, he thought piously, he had to make sure that she wouldn't enter into a relationship with the wrong man for the wrong reasons. Her eventual fate meant nothing to him but he was, he decided, not without conscience.

'Would you like to tell me that no man has ever made you feel like I just did?' Theo asked lazily.

'I most certainly would not.' No man *had*. Thank God he wasn't a mind-reader. 'And we have to get up. We can't stay here all day.'

'Why not? Are you expecting visitors?'

'No, but…'

'Mm. I know. It's wildly decadent, isn't it?' he murmured, amused. 'Lying here in bed during the day…Admittedly we'll have to get dressed some time and get ourselves something to eat… Unless, of course, you have stuff in your kitchen, in which case we can just stroll out there as we are and eat… Now *that* would be wildly decadent…'

'You're teasing.' Sophie blushed because the thought of doing that did seem very debauched indeed, which said a great deal, she thought ruefully, about her wildly exciting life. While twenty-somethings all over the country spent their free time strolling around kitchens with their lovers in the nude, here she was, as buttoned up as a fifty-year-old spinster.

Curiosity, as sharp as a blade, slashed through her. Did he do this often? Take time out during the day to make love? Lie in bed with a woman, only getting up to eat? What women? How many had there been? Why was there no woman around now?

Sophie fought down the urge to ask him any of those things. Something inside her recognised that her burgeoning curiosity could blossom into a dangerous need to get to know him and getting to know him was not part of her plan. As it was, she already knew too much about him. Not in the detail but in the general—the fact that he could be as amusing and witty as he could be arrogant, that his arrogance, even, had a certain compelling charm, that his intelligence outstripped that of any man she had ever known, possibly even her father, whom she had always considered head and shoulders above the rest of the human race as far as brain power went.

'I'm going to have a bath,' she said abruptly, slipping her legs off the side of the bed.

'I'll come.' Holding on to her was like trying to hold water in the palm of his hand. Right now, Theo could feel her beginning to slip through his fingers and he wasn't going to let it happen. Touching her, making love with her, had left him wanting more. He also needed to find out what the position was with Robert, whom he saw as not so much a threat as an unnecessary irritation.

'I can bathe myself,' Sophie was telling him, trying to maintain an appropriate distance and hating the little swirl of excitement that sparked through her as she contemplated the luxury of being bathed by this big powerful man.

She could feel little goosebumps on her arms as the warmth of the bed and their shared space was replaced by the coldness of the flat into which heat was only now slowly beginning to creep.

'Sit.'

Theo dwarfed the tiny bathroom. Sophie could barely look at his towering frame. Suddenly, she felt very vulnerable, sitting as commanded on the toilet seat while he ran a bath, testing the water and pouring in bath salts, one hundred per cent comfortable with his nakedness. Her new role as decadent woman of the world obviously was confined to the bedroom. Once out of the bedroom, she seemed to revert to her usual self, anxiously wondering whether she had done the right thing.

'Stop it right now,' Theo said, without looking at her.

'Stop what?'

'Chewing your lip, folding your arms across your breasts, thinking about what happened between us like a dog worrying a bone.' He turned around to face her, all man. He walked towards her and gently prised her arms from their predictably folded position so that he could look at her breasts in unashamed appreciation. She had glorious breasts. He could stand for hours and feast his eyes on the sight. He knelt down in front of her and cupped them with his hands, feeling their weight and hearing the alteration in her breathing as she responded. Amazingly, he could take her again. Instead, he steadied himself and dragged his eyes from the tightening peaks of her nipples.

'Hop in.'

Sophie could feel his eyes burning through her as she walked to the bath and stepped into the water, which was just the right temperature.

'So much better in a bigger bath,' Theo murmured. 'I could get in with you…'

'And do you?' Sophie asked. 'Get into baths with women?'

'No, not as a general rule.' He got the bath sponge and

began washing her neck, then, as she leaned forward, her back. It was a dreamy experience. Sophie closed her eyes and sat up so that her breasts were exposed and he could rub the soapy sponge over them. 'Now stand up.'

Sophie obeyed, eyes still dreamily half closed. The sensation of being rubbed all over with warm soapy water was intensely exquisite. And he took his time, frequently squeezing the sponge and dipping it back into the bath water, paying attention to every inch of her, parting her legs so that over and over he could rub the sponge just there, on her most intimate part, on that throbbing nub, until her body was screaming for satisfaction.

Never, *never*, not even in the deepest recesses of her mind, had Sophie ever imagined that she could achieve orgasm like this, in full view of a man's eyes, shamelessly juddering until every ounce of pleasure had been squeezed from her and then releasing one long breath of deep satisfaction.

She looked at him as he got to his feet and leaned forward to kiss her. He had seen her enjoy her most intimate experience and she wasn't horrified at the thought. In fact, she smiled and told him very nearly what he wanted to hear, which was that this was the most pleasurable bath she had ever had. She wound her arms around his neck. 'And I'm going to return the favour, never you fear.'

It was a little under an hour later by the time they emerged, sated, from the bathroom and Sophie's eyes were glowing. Lunch was something they threw together—bread and cheese and, in keeping with the unconventional nature of the day, a bottle of wine. And they talked, Theo stepping over certain topics, encouraging her to open up so that he could broach the topic of Robert, which had been temporarily set to one side.

Eventually, in an atmosphere of domesticity which Theo succumbed to because it was a one-off, and with mugs of coffee set in front of them as they sat in the small sitting room, cosy, warm and content, he tentatively broached the subject of her relationship with Robert. In an oblique fashion. And he watched her as she spoke, lazily playing with her hair, maintaining a physical contact that his body seemed to crave.

'I'm a possessive lover,' he told her. 'I can't say I even like the thought of another man looking at my woman.'

My woman. It had a glorious ring to it until Sophie reminded herself that this was a blip on the horizon, two ships meeting in the night, soon to go their separate ways.

'Robert's just a friend at the moment,' she said, tucking her feet under his thigh and resting back on the arm of the sofa.

Theo didn't like the sound of *at the moment* even though he was quick to acknowledge in his head that her future dealings with the man were not his concern. This was passion born of the moment and with a predetermined time span.

'Just like this is simply something that's happened at the moment,' she added, squashing the feeling of sharp regret that washed over her. 'I think we both know where we stand,' she continued, determined to make sure that she drove the point home, that he needn't fear that she would become wrapped up in him. She was a modern woman, able to handle a modern relationship, which meant wonderful, passionate, fulfilling sex with no questions asked. She was well aware that his departure date was in her diary, with a two-week break before a couple and their two children rented the cottage for a week over the New Year period.

Robert, she knew now beyond any doubt, was never going to be a contender to her heart and she would tell him, but why should she let Theo know that? Didn't modern women have their secrets? And some instinct she never knew she had warned her to hold back.

'Enjoy the moment,' Theo murmured, pulling her towards him so that she was lying against his chest, hearing the thud of his heart.

'I never thought I would do that,' Sophie confessed. 'I mean, have a relationship with a man and be perfectly happy that it was going nowhere…'

'But you can with me…' Why was it that he didn't like to hear that? She also wasn't ruling Robert out of her life, which he would have liked—yet another illogical thought that he pushed away.

'Mmm.' She squirmed round to straddle him and clasped her hands behind his neck. They had both changed, he into his boxer shorts and nothing else, she into a T-shirt and underwear. Just enough to preserve propriety, which she had insisted on, much to his amusement as he would have been happy to stroll through the flat in the nude. 'No tomorrow.'

'Oh, I think tomorrow is a certainty,' Theo drawled, cupping her rear with his hands. 'In fact, I can think of quite a few things we could do tomorrow…'

'Yes—' Sophie laughed '—your writing and my work!' But the temptation to bunk off reared its ugly head and held her captive.

'Our work…' Theo said, tilting her face so that she was looking at him, green eyes tangled with brown. 'I'm going to install that program, Sophie, whether you like it or not, so you'll have to put your pride in a cupboard and bring it out some other day.'

'You won't have time—I don't want to interfere with your writing.'

'Don't worry about…about that…' he told her. 'I'll find it

relaxing. Of course, I shall have to lay down a few provisions which I consider essential to my successful programming…' He felt her laugh into his chest and a thrill of intense satisfaction snaked through him. Satisfaction and…peace.

'And that would be…?'

'Oh, sex in unusual places and possibly at odd times… Walks on the beach so that we can talk about work and computers and other stimulating topics like that… You cooking at least one meal for me without anything on…' He wondered where that last had come from but, having said it, he already felt turned on at the thought of her ladling food on to his plate while he watched the sexy movement of her bewitching body. With a disturbing leap of imagination, he thought that that request would never have been on the agenda with Elena. She had aroused other things in him but certainly not this fierce desire rushing like burning acid through his veins. But already Sophie was distracting him from following the thought through, teasing him, reminding him how much there was to life outside the work that had dominated his for so many months, showing him his humanity.

Right now, right here. That was all that mattered. Accustomed to controlling the course of his life and a future that was as ruthlessly marshalled as was humanly possible, Theo allowed himself the unique indulgence of just going with the flow.

CHAPTER SEVEN

SOPHIE knew that she was playing with fire. She felt it every time she was in his company, every time those amazing green eyes lazily skimmed over her, every time his hands skilfully caressed her yearning body. Even when there was no physical contact between them when they were just strolling through the town, wrapped up in layers of clothing to combat the fierce winter cold, she was still tantalisingly aware of the dangerous edge of her attraction.

Theo Andreou was not the kind of man with whom she should be having a relationship. Yes, there was a lot to be said for reckless abandon. After all, just the one life, why waste it in relentless pursuit of what was right, when a little bit of wrong could be so much fun? Two consenting adults enjoying each other.

When Sophie thought about it like that, she could convince her uneasy conscience that she was doing the right thing.

But, more and more, small nasty thoughts were beginning to mar the unblemished surface of their easy, no strings attached relationship.

When she wasn't with him, she longed for him, wondered about a future that was not on the cards and discovered that the only way to deal with the eventuality of not seeing him once his time was up was to shove it out of her mind. There was a steady little voice in her head telling her that she had to give it up, that the likes of Theo were out of her league, but that too she could silence.

She told herself that it was fine, that the little vacuum they had created around themselves as one week turned into two and two into three and three into four was absolutely wonderful. It was, she consoled herself, the way modern young people enjoyed life. No old-fashioned inconvenient soul-searching, no desperate questions about marriage and commitment, just a lazy, enjoyable amble with another person for as long as it lasted.

And Theo never gave her any indication that things wouldn't come crashing down as soon as he left Cornwall.

Like an addict enjoying something taboo, Sophie could recognise the dangerous shortcomings of her situation and still remain locked in her cycle of just wanting more of the same.

However, tonight she intended to broach at least one tricky question. It helped that they would be having dinner out. She had realised early on that just one touch from him could send all her thoughts and good intentions scattering to the four winds.

She took one last look at herself in the mirror just to make sure that she passed muster, not that Theo ever gave her any indication that she was anything but beautiful. Indeed, he had the ability to make her feel very special, literally as though he had eyes only for her, which she knew was simply a gift of his because she certainly wasn't a supermodel in the making.

Tonight she was wearing a long brown skirt, which she had teamed up with a terracotta polo-necked ribbed jumper and her brown boots. All of the items had seen better days, but with a wardrobe severely constrained by financial limits she fancied she had made the most of things. A bit of mixing and matching, a couple of bright scarves and some cheap costume jewellery and a tiny bit of magic could be created. At any rate, that was how Theo made her feel. Magical.

Sophie laughed at the silly notion and headed out.

Outside it was freezing cold, with a savage wind that cut through her coat and clamped its teeth all the way through her layers of clothes until she could feel her eyes burning. Normally, Theo would have collected her in his car but she had wanted to meet him at the restaurant. Every so often, in one of her more lucid moments, she would fight off the demons of her addiction and push herself into a more detached position. Tonight had been one of those times, although it had taken a great deal of effort not to be persuaded by him that she was being silly, turning down the warmth of his car in favour of public transport, which was never that reliable during the winter months.

She arrived, after a combination of her feet and the bus, at the restaurant to find Theo ensconced by the bar and watching the door with a scowl.

It was one of the more popular restaurants locally, with a vibrant atmosphere and a price list that would normally have put it way out of her range. She wondered how Theo had been able to book a table for them at such short notice, but she had discovered that the man had an unusual knack for getting his own way.

'I told you that you should have come with me,' he growled as soon as she had been divested of her coat, scarf and gloves and sat on the stool next to him.

'That's a nice way to greet me,' Sophie teased him, 'when you haven't seen me for a couple of days.' That had been another concerted effort on her part to try and make contact with the independence she seemed to be leaving behind at great speed. She had spent two nights with some of her university friends and, aside from the fact that she had thought constantly about Theo, she had had a great time.

'It's freezing out there,' Theo said, ignoring her interruption. 'You'll end up in hospital with pneumonia. I suppose you caught the bus instead of taking a cab?'

'There's no need to worry about me, Theo,' Sophie told him, leaning one elbow on the bar and watching his face with great pleasure. 'I'm accustomed to taking buses. Some of us are.'

'You're not going to go into your rant about the haves and the have-nots, are you?'

'I'd prefer to have a glass of wine, but if you want me to start ranting…'

Theo grinned reluctantly, already feeling himself relax after what had been a pretty stressful day. Three calls from a woman who had been chasing him before he'd left, despite his evident lack of interest, inviting him to a Christmas do. Gloria had obviously given her the cottage number, maybe thinking that he needed a break from his solitude. He would have to have a word with her about that.

And then two tricky meetings in Hong Kong were looming. They could just about wait until after Christmas, but the prospect of normality and all that it entailed had put him in a foul mood.

To make matters worse, Sophie had been away, enjoying herself and doing God only knew what. She could veer between utter openness and infuriating detachment with an ease that brought out the worst in him.

'How did you manage to get a table here?' she was asking, looking around her at the butterflies that had emerged from all corners of the county, dressed in their finery. Theo, dressed in a simple pair of dark trousers and one of his cream Ralph Lauren shirts, looked totally in keeping with the crowd. Which made her wonder aloud at her own garb, which in turn led to the light hearted banter that had become part and parcel of their relationship. She felt so comfortable with him and yet was so keenly aware of his unsuitability. Why? Because he was so wildly out of her orbit? Or because she knew that the information he dispensed about himself was vaguely inadequate, said so much yet not enough?

Their table was in a prime position at the back of the restaurant. They had a bird's eye view of the other diners while being virtually invisible to prying eyes, thanks to a row of lush plants that hemmed the table in at one side.

Theo watched her as she wondered how he had managed to acquire such a desirable spot. Of course, if she asked, he would shrug and make some vaguely amusing remark about the power of his charm. The last thing he would do would be to tell her the truth, which was that his promise to the manager of the purchase of an extremely expensive celebratory bottle of champagne had swung it in his favour. That and, of course, his presence. People generally obliged him by doing what he wanted and Jean Luc, the manager of the little French restaurant, had been no exception.

Sophie, he had come to realise, seemed oblivious to the fact that he was clearly immensely well off. Tonight, he knew, she would offer to go halves on the bill and it would be just as well that her menu would not carry prices. He would tell her that it was really less than he might have expected and bring out the old-fashioned assertion that as a gentleman she should humour him by accepting his generosity in the manner in which it was meant.

He used that excuse a lot. Sometimes she bought it, other

times she insisted on giving him money and, whenever he possibly could, he slipped the money back into her bag when her attention was somewhere else.

And, unlike any woman he had ever met, she never expected anything from him. Several times over the course of the weeks, as they had strolled through one of the towns, he had offered to buy her something she had seen in passing, something she had liked, usually something of an antique nature. She had refused every single time. He wondered whether it was her nature and dismissed the notion as quickly as it had formed in his head. There was no woman on the face of the earth who would not accept gifts from a man. He decided that Sophie was no different. It was just that she had no real idea as to the enormity of his wealth. If she had, then yes, she would happily have taken. He convinced himself that it was just as well they would be parting company in due course. That way, he would never suffer the disillusionment of finding out that her feet were made of clay.

And their parting was going to be sooner rather than later. Time was flying by at an unholy speed.

'Hello? Is anybody there?' Sophie, watching Theo's distant expression, felt a chill of fear and she wondered whether this was the start of him losing interest in her. She had been discussing some minor bit of village gossip, a ridiculous piece of nonsense concerning a couple just sitting by the window at the far side of the room. Of course, he would be bored rigid by her anecdote.

'You were miles away, Theo,' she said.

'Oh, was I…?' He gave her one of his long, slow smiles, tempted to tell her that when he was in her company there was never a second when he wasn't supremely, ridiculously one hundred per cent focused on her, even if it didn't appear so.

'Is that why I know exactly what you were saying about Jane and Henry Glover and their little slice of scandal?'

Sophie grinned back at him, foolishly relieved and even more foolishly happy when he reached across the table to capture her hand in his.

Sometimes she almost felt as though they really had something that could go somewhere, that their relationship might really function beyond the artificial life span imposed upon it. This was one of those moments. Here they were, having dinner in an absolutely gorgeous restaurant which was festive with the colours of Christmas. In the corner of the room a fully decorated Christmas tree lent an air of excited expectation and outside the air was heavy with the promise of snow. How much better could it get? And when he looked at her like that, as if he could read deep into her soul, she couldn't help but have the delirious feeling that maybe he felt as much for her as she did for him.

Which, she suddenly thought, was *what*?

The image of herself as a modern day twenty-first century woman, enjoying a relationship that was going nowhere but immense fun nevertheless, floated through the window like a vanishing puff of smoke.

In its place was left the much truer picture of herself as a woman in love. She didn't eagerly look forward to seeing him and miss him when she wasn't with him because she was physically attracted to his body! Nor did she find herself laughing at the things he said, confiding in him, wanting to share every bit of herself with him, because *he was sexy*. She was a different woman in his presence because she had done the unthinkable and had fallen in love with him.

Sophie could feel the colour drain from her face and, just when she needed rescuing most, it came in the format of their starters, which were brought to the table in style. Along with a bottle of champagne, which was ceremoniously opened with a loud popping of the cork.

Several people stared round at their table, smiling, and she wondered what they might be thinking. Perhaps that the couple they were looking at were celebrating something momentous?

Maybe, she thought on a wild surge of optimism, *they were*! She smiled, blushing, at Theo and raised her glass in a toast to Christmas, quietly thinking that perhaps, just perhaps, this wonderful champagne was an outward symbol of what his unconscious mind was telling him, that there *was* something to celebrate, that theirs wasn't just some passing affair but something real and substantial and *worth celebrating*!

'This food,' he said, in between mouthfuls of his starter, 'is as good as anything I've ever tasted in London.'

'Tell me about where you live.' Every time they had touched briefly on his life, he had veered the conversation away. Sophie was determined that that would not happen this time. She wanted to find out everything about this man who had captured her heart against her will. He knew so much more about her than she did about him and his life was, paradoxically, just *so much more interesting*! Crazy, but underneath that peculiarly enchanting arrogance was obviously a streak of real modesty.

'You know where I live,' Theo said abruptly.

'Yes. In London. But what's your house like?'

Talking about London and his life there reminded Theo of the grim reality awaiting him in under three weeks. He had not actually planned on staying in the cottage as long as he had, intending on a minimum rest period, sufficiently long enough to satisfy his mother but not a minute beyond. As it was, he was still here and intended to enjoy the remainder of his stay without any thoughts of his London life. But Sophie did not give up easily and he reluctantly answered her questions as briefly as he could. He lived in a very modern apartment, size and location undisclosed. He laughed when she teased him about the cottage, wondering aloud how he could enjoy something so different from what he was used to.

'Variety is the spice of life,' he said, sitting back and watching her mobile, expressive face.

'I'd love to live in London, at least for a while,' Sophie said wistfully.

'You'd hate it.'

Sophie, cruising along on the rosy image of them exploring London together, taking a few steps further to discovering themselves, was brought abruptly back down to earth by the finality of his voice.

'Why do you say that?' she asked. Their starters had been taken away. She could see the waitress weaving her way to their table with their main courses just when she didn't want to be interrupted, just when she was on the brink of justifying exactly why a dose of London could be very salutary for her, never mind the workload still waiting to be done. Her momentum to get her father's affairs sorted had recently lost its urgency. Really, the rent from the cottage was managing to tide over the baying creditors, at least some of them, and she couldn't be bothered to worry about the rest.

'It's crowded, polluted and lonely.'

'In which case, why do you live there?' She sat back while the waitress placed their dishes in front of them and then leaned towards him, her face alight with lively curiosity.

'Because I've become accustomed to crowds, pollution and loneliness.'

Sophie laughed and tucked into her food. She couldn't

imagine Theo ever being lonely. He was too charismatic for that.

'You, on the other hand, are accustomed to wide open spaces and beautiful scenery.'

'But variety is the spice of life.' Sophie threw his quote back at him and he nodded an appreciative touché. 'Not that Cornwall isn't absolutely perfect sometimes. I mean, it's beautiful in winter.' She hesitated and then looked him squarely in the eye. 'Which brings me to Christmas Day. Are you intending to return to London? I expect you have friends and family you'd like to share the day with…'

Sophie held her breath. This was the question she had left the flat intending to ask and she superstitiously felt that the right answer would be an indication of whether they were going anywhere or not. If he chose to stay or else invited her to go to London with him, then maybe there was a future. She didn't think of the alternative.

Theo looked at her for a long time in silence. His mother wanted him back in Greece for Christmas, as did all the members of his extended family, most of whom he only saw very occasionally. His friends had issued invitations, largely expecting them to be turned down. Christmas Day, Theo strongly felt, was a family day and, whereas he had usually returned to Greece for a couple of days over the period, he had little inclination to do so this year. Nor did he fancy a holiday on his own doing one of the high risk sports that had so absorbed him over the past few months. Less desirable was the thought of spending it in the company of the woman who had called several times and seemed intent on netting him for some festive fun.

In fact, just at this point in time, nothing seemed more inviting than staying put. And, face it, he told himself, they were having fun on borrowed time. Why not go the whole nine yards?

He shook his head slowly, thoughtfully, and Sophie felt her stomach flip over with joy. 'Are you sure?' she asked with a trace of anxiety because no good fortune came without a catch, but he was nodding, still telling her that the clean air, the restful lifestyle, would do him good, that everything else could be put on hold for just a bit.

Sophie shut her mind firmly against the enticing sound of wedding bells and the pitter-patter of tiny feet. Such thoughts were madness, given the nature of the man, but a thread of hope uncurled inside her. They would spend Christmas together, go shopping together for Christmas lunch, put up a tree, which was something she had not contemplated doing in her grief after her father's death. And then, afterwards... Well, she would cross that bridge when she came to it, but surely the fact that he was willing to spend such an important occasion with her was indication enough of some kind of commitment, whatever he might have said in the past to the contrary.

She spent the remainder of the evening floating on a cloud. She even edged the conversation around to a Christmas tree and was pleased when he expanded a bit on his past, telling her about his Christmases spent as a boy and, latterly, about what they did in Greece over the festive season.

When she looked, the bottle of champagne was finished and most of the tables were empty. And when, still floating on that cloud, they left the restaurant, it was to find that the promise of snow had turned into reality. Nothing dramatic. Just small flakes blowing about like the petals of flowers.

Theo led her to where his car was parked and informed her that she would spend the night at the cottage.

Sophie, with half a bottle of champagne inside her, had no problem with that. In fact, she couldn't wait.

And nor, she thought with a satisfied thrill, could he. The

car screeched to a halt outside the cottage and by the time the front door was shut behind them, his coat and jacket had been discarded and he was untucking the shirt from the waistband of his trousers.

Sophie had still not become accustomed to the sight of his naked body, the sheer masculine beauty of it. She knew that he found her fascination amusing; in fact, he had told her so on a number of occasions, but she just couldn't seem to stop herself from staring.

They reached the bedroom just as they had both shed their final item of clothing, leaving a trail of discarded clothes behind them. Later on, Sophie would gather them up, but for now her pulses were racing with intoxicating anticipation.

Every time they made love was like a new and wonderful revelation of excitement, but tonight was different. Tonight, she could feel an exquisite tenderness to their lovemaking and she wondered whether he could as well.

She knew where, for her, the difference lay. Nothing to do with the physical act which, as he moved against her, touching with his hands, his fingers, his mouth, his tongue, was as fulfilling as it always was. The difference this time lay in the fact that she had discovered how she truly felt about him and love had released in her a new dimension to their passion.

Afterwards, spent, she rolled over on to her side and linked her fingers around his neck.

'Are you happy?' she murmured, still basking in the afterglow of knowing that he wanted to spend Christmas Day in her company.

Theo frowned at the question and wondered where that had come from, although, when he considered it, he was, he thought, happy at this point in time. A remarkable achievement, given everything that had happened.

Still…it seemed an odd question and he was contemplating how to answer it when they heard the banging of the knocker on the front door. It was loud enough to rouse the county, or so it seemed in the dead of a winter's night in the middle of nowhere, but instead of Theo and Sophie leaping out of bed in immediate response, they stared at each other in mutual bewilderment.

'Someone doesn't realise that the cottage has been rented out,' Theo said dryly. A sudden thought crossed his mind and he didn't like it. 'If it's the ex, get rid of him.'

Ever since Theo had appeared on the scene, Sophie had gradually eased away from Robert. Her excuse, initially, had been that she needed time to think about his proposal, then later, when he had pressed her for an answer, she had delayed the inevitable, guiltily aware that she should make a clean break but not wanting to hurt his feelings any more than she already had.

What could be more ego crushing for a man than to know that the woman he had planned on marrying was more interested in a random stranger she hadn't known for longer than ten minutes?

It had been a relief when, a few days ago, he'd told her that he would be staying with his parents again. It had also been a huge relief that he hadn't mentioned a thing about marriage and the pitter-patter of tiny feet. Not a word.

Naturally, she had been vague when Theo had asked her where Robert was. Moreover, he had assumed, the minute their relationship became physical, that wherever he was it was nowhere near her, and she had gone along with the assumption because really it was technically correct. Cheltenham was nowhere near Cornwall. Nor had she wanted to give Theo the satisfaction of knowing that he had been responsible for the other man's departure from her life. Saying neither one thing nor the other, she had kept her options open.

Now, of course, if it was indeed Robert downstairs—and who else could it be at the ludicrous time of twelve-fifteen in the early hours of the morning—she would make her choice once and for all and with Theo there as witness.

To her, it seemed as though she had taken forever to work through things in her head. In reality, she was out of the bed within seconds of the knocker being struck and pulling on Theo's towelling robe, which he kept on a hook behind the bedroom door.

'I'll handle this,' she told him. 'Please don't make a scene.'

'Depends on how you handle the situation,' Theo grated, reaching into the cupboard and slinging on the first thing that came to hand, which was a pair of boxer shorts and a T-shirt.

He had known in his gut that the man hadn't disappeared off the scene, at least not in any sense that mattered. But, actually, he had convinced himself that it was of no concern one way or the other. He and Sophie were enjoying a brief fling and, while they were together, he expected—no, *demanded*—that he be the only man in her life, but he could hardly force her to dismiss the other man entirely to accommodate their brief liaison.

Hearing the banging on the door and imagining her ex back on the scene creating the rumpus, Theo realised that he damn well cared that she hadn't ditched the guy for good.

Sophie was aware of him following hot on her heels as she dashed towards the front door. She was convinced that everyone in the village would be able to hear the racket and she couldn't face a barrage of sidelong looks when she went to buy her bread in the morning.

Actually, even if *everyone* in the village hadn't heard the banging, it only took *one* passer-by to have heard and it more or less came to the same thing. She realised, with a start, that life in the little village where she had grown up no longer held the charms it once had when her father was alive. He had been the anchor keeping her rooted firmly to her birth place. With him gone and no relatives to carry the torch, there was no reason for her to stay. Yes, there was the familiarity of being a known quantity, of going into shops and being able to pass the time of day with people who had known you from child-hood, but at the age of twenty-six familiarity seemed a poor relation compared to excitement.

Excitement was London. The big city. Excitement was Theo. She would tell Robert, once and for all and in Theo's hearing, that whatever flimsy relationship they had had was now over, that there was no way she could marry him. She might even throw in her decision to leave Cornwall as soon as her father's affairs were wrapped up, to move to London. She could easily complete her teacher training course there. She was certain of it. She would plant the seeds of possibil-ity in Theo's head. The possibility that their relationship might carry on beyond the confines of his stay in Cornwall. The possibility that she might become a part of his life in London.

'Just get rid of him.' Theo gripped her arm, drawing her to a halt. 'You should never have kept him hanging on. We both know that you don't feel anything for him.'

'Of course I *feel something for Robert*!' Sophie defended heatedly.

'You like him.' Theo shrugged but his eyes were burning holes through her. 'I like my tailor but it doesn't mean that I'm going to marry him.'

'*You have a tailor?*' Sophie asked, distracted by that throw-away piece of information. 'How on earth does a writer afford *a tailor*? Perhaps I should pack in the teacher training and do a creative writing course instead!'

One loud bang silenced them both and Sophie flew towards the front door. She felt agitated and curiously excited at the prospects lying just ahead, the shimmer of possibilities not yet taken up, a whisper in her ear that suggested the un-thinkable might just come to pass—Theo might just, without even realising it, feel for her strongly enough to want what they had to continue.

She pulled open the door and froze as the wind and cold blew in the end of her dreams.

Later, when she would try to recall that precise moment, she would wonder who was the more surprised at the person swept into the flagstoned hallway on a rain-filled gust of freezing wind. Theo's sharp intake of breath reflected his surprise and then they both asked, in the same breath, 'Who are you?' and, 'What the hell are *you* doing here?'

The six foot blonde woman, wrapped from neck to ankle in a cream fur coat, glanced briefly in Sophie's direction before focusing her huge blue eyes on Theo. She looked ab-solutely livid.

'I've spent *hours* trying to find this place!'

Sophie shut the door but remained on the periphery of the picture, with her back pressed against the door and feeling utterly inadequate in a towelling robe. Which the other woman seemed not to have noticed at all in her haste to escape the biting cold.

Then something clicked and the blonde turned around very slowly until she was staring at Sophie. Then at Theo. Then back to Sophie. All of this in the space of just a few confused seconds, during which time the silence was electric.

Theo was the first to break the silence and this time his voice was deadly cold when he repeated his question.

'I came…' the blonde woman said, 'to look for *you*. I *thought* you might have wanted some company over the Christmas period. Obviously I was *wrong*! Obviously, poor, grieving man that you are, you have managed to find yourself a little local lass for company!'

'Who *are* you?' Sophie asked, thoroughly confused now.

Six foot of towering blonde beauty fixed cold blue eyes on her. The woman was clearly a model, from the perfection of her dead straight blonde hair, which had managed to remain sleek even after a tussle with the elements, to the tips of her inappropriately tan-booted feet.

'I don't believe you were invited here, Yvonne. There is a bed and breakfast in the village. I will book you in and you can drive back to London first thing in the morning. A wasted trip for you, I'm afraid.' His voice was brutally cold and Sophie saw the other woman flinch as though she had been struck.

Was this the same funny, warm, sexy man with whom she had just made wild, abandoned love? Speaking in this hard, flat voice? A voice that sent a shiver of apprehension running down her spine?

And who the hell was this strikingly beautiful woman? An ex? Or a current lover she knew nothing about?

Sophie suddenly realised the gaps in her knowledge of the man she had fallen in love with. The scant amount of information he had supplied about his past. Certainly no mention of a towering blonde who looked as though she would sit nicely on the cover of Vogue magazine. Convenient lapse in memory, that.

'I'm Sophie.' She held out her hand and the blonde returned the handshake more out of surprise at the gesture, Sophie reckoned, than anything else. 'And you are…?' She was very much aware of Theo looking at her, running his fingers through his black hair, his expression a mixture of frustration and anger.

'Yvonne Shulz.'

'Come through. I'll make you a cup of tea…'

CHAPTER EIGHT

SOPHIE had not set any alarm, but she was awake the following morning by eight-thirty. Her body had obviously taken its cue from her mind and set its own alarm, knowing that she would be going to the cottage to see Theo to have her questions answered.

Of course, they should have been answered the night before and, yes, some of them had, but not all.

Sophie thought back to Yvonne and the scene that had followed with a little shudder of pure horror. She had wanted to ask her a hundred things but Theo had had other ideas and hanging around like a spare part while his ex-girlfriend, or whoever she was, had an intimate one-to-one session with his current lover had not featured high on his agenda.

Thinking back, Sophie couldn't quite understand how he had managed it, but manage it he had—to get Yvonne out of the cottage without raising his voice. She had protested, but not for long. It had only been when the tears had also failed to summon up a response that she'd turned to Sophie and delivered the information that had still succeeded in wrecking the little fairy tale cloud-cuckoo-land she had stupidly built for herself.

Theo wasn't a writer! Sophie couldn't quite remember

what company he owned, or maybe it was a whole lot of companies, but he was a very rich, very important man in London with women at his beck and call. Except—and this was where it had become a little confusing because at this point Yvonne had been very firmly on her way back to her car, enraged at her dismissal—Theo wasn't involved with anyone because he was off women.

Yvonne had spat that out in a voice that dripped acidity, which made Sophie wonder what exactly the other woman had meant by the remark.

In fact, she had spent much of her night wondering what the remark had meant. Why had Theo retreated to the middle of nowhere under the phoney guise of being a *writer*? Because he had doubts about his sexuality and he needed a rest from the bevy of beautiful women who apparently had nothing better to do in London than chase behind him? Well, yes, she had thought bitterly, that *would* test a man who was confused about his sexuality! She couldn't quite see what *her* role was in this theory but maybe she didn't have a role as such, maybe she was just someone to fill a gap while he floated around in a muddle.

She could have kicked herself for having fallen for his cover story about *being a writer*. Sure, there had been no reason not to have taken him at his word, but really, how many times had she marvelled at how *little* he lived up to her expectations of what a writer should be?

Sophie stared up at the ceiling and tried to calm herself by taking deep breaths.

He had frogmarched Yvonne to the car, piling her in, making her wait for him while he got his coat so that he could drive her to the nearest bed and breakfast. Over his shoulder, he had told Sophie to go back to her place, that it was too late to begin long-winded discussions, that she could come back in the morning.

Sophie had looked at him and barely recognised the man she loved. He was a stranger. A stranger with a strange past who had deliberately lied to her.

She squeezed her eyes shut tight and clenched her fists. Half of her wanted to leave this flat, lock the door behind her and disappear until he was no longer around. The other half needed to find out just what was going on. She had been a fool, of that there was no question, but she needed to find out just how big a fool she had been.

The only glimmer of brightness on the horizon was the fact that she had never told him anything about wanting to carry on with their relationship after he had returned to London.

Thinking how close she had come to revealing to him how she felt made her feel sick inside.

It was after nine before Sophie finally dragged herself out of bed. When she looked outside the window, it was to discover that the snow was heavier than it had been the night before. The ground wasn't blanketed in Christmas card white, but it was getting that way. The temperature had dropped and the snow was sticking. Lord only knew how the hapless Yvonne was going to get back up to London but then, Sophie thought bitterly, Theo being a rich man, he could arrange anything. He probably had his own private helicopter on standby for circumstances just like that! Urgent transportation of stranded and unwanted female in the middle of nowhere!

He had told her, curtly, that he would be in all day. Sophie wasn't going to wait, though. She would go and see him and when she left, she would leave for good. Let him contact the estate agent if he needed anything, or else he could always go through Catherine or Annie. There would be no need for her to see him and she had no intention of doing so. She just needed to have her questions answered so that she could bring closure to the whole unfortunate episode.

She dressed warmly, lots of layers, and finished with her black coat. It would be soaked through by the time she made it to the cottage but her waterproof coat was *at* the cottage, forgotten there a while back after one of their blissful excursions into the town followed by the warmth of the bedroom and their bodies so in tune with one another.

For the first time, she dreaded seeing him. Indeed, the closer she got to the cottage, the more her steps began to slow and she had to take several deep breaths to steady herself by the time she finally made it there.

The snow had gathered apace. Like it or not, she couldn't stand outside the cottage indefinitely, trying to screw up her courage to face him. If she did, she would end up in hospital with pneumonia. She breathed in deeply and half ran up to the front door and banged on it, just like Yvonne had banged on it the night before.

Theo answered almost immediately and she was uncharitably gratified to notice that he was looking a little the worse for wear. She didn't dwell on it, though, choosing to brush past him, straight into the hallway, where she promptly turned, hands still shoved into the deep pockets of her coat, and looked at him expressionlessly.

'Did you manage to sort Yvonne out for the night?' Sophie asked politely and Theo scowled darkly at her.

'You don't have to be so bloody polite, Sophie. It's not as though we don't know one another…'

'Oh, but we don't, do we?' She couldn't have hoped for a better cue to make her remember why she was standing where she was, feeling as she did.

'Look, let's go into the kitchen. Have you eaten any break-fast? I haven't. I've had one hell of a night.'

'Poor Theo. Nasty when your past jumps up and grabs you by the throat, I imagine.' Her voice was cold as ice and saccharine-sweet.

Theo didn't answer. He stalked off towards the kitchen, once again the intruder in her domain, and after a few seconds Sophie reluctantly followed him.

The hardest thing was the pain of comparison, the anguish of remembering how many times they had sat at the kitchen table, sharing conversation, touching one another. The same kitchen table at which she now perched, having removed her coat and left it hanging over the banister in the hall.

She watched as he made a pot of coffee and didn't say anything when he placed a mug in front of her before sitting at the opposite end of the table.

'Why did you bother to come here if you dislike me so much?' he asked, watching her over the rim of his mug as he sipped some of his coffee.

'I needed to find out to whom I've rented my cottage. Precisely.'

'Because you think I might skip the last payment?'

'Oh, no. Not that,' Sophie said acidly. 'Why would you skip the last payment when you're apparently Mr Money is No Object? You could probably buy this cottage several times over, never mind rent it out for a couple of months!' She struggled to bite back tears of hurt, regret and bitterness. Every word was like the slash of a razor somewhere deep inside her and she couldn't look at him at all, couldn't see that sexy, beautiful face which had made her bones turn to water and which had melted her heart.

'I won't apologise for having money.'

'I'm not asking you to! I just want to know why you lied to me! Why concoct some stupid story about being a writer, of all things?' She gave a hollow laugh and stared down at the coffee.

'It…wasn't my intention,' Theo said heavily. He stood up and moved to stand by the kitchen sink, leaning against the counter, arms folded. Lord, she looked broken and he couldn't blame her. She had discovered in the very worst possible way that he was not the man he had pretended to be.

He had to put distance between them because his need was to go over to where she was sitting and kneel by her chair, take her hand and of course there was no way he could do that. For starters, she would probably brain him and, also, if he took her hand he would have to tell her that everything was going to be all right, and that would have been yet another lie because everything wasn't going to be all right. Things weren't going to return to their even keel.

For the hundredth time he cursed Yvonne. She had been persistent in London and he should have shaken her off in a more determined fashion. Instead, he had been polite, vaguely dodging her requests that they meet up, using excuses instead of telling her straight off the bat that he wasn't interested.

Maybe, psychologically, he had already been toying with the notion of moving on with his life. Maybe he had just been lazy, never thinking that she would pursue him in the face of his polite evasions.

He had spent much of the night reliving that moment when Sophie had pulled open the front door. He could even recall exactly what he'd been thinking at the time—that it was surely going to be her ex. He could remember the ugly stirrings of jealousy he had felt.

Seeing Yvonne had been a shock. She had telephoned him,

had left a couple of messages, but no hint that she'd intended making her way down to the cottage.

'No?' Sophie said, raising her eyebrows. 'You mean it happened against your will? You never intended to fabricate a career for yourself but, in conversation with the estate agent, you suddenly found your mouth taking over?'

'I didn't book this cottage,' Theo confessed heavily. 'In fact, I'd never been to this part of the world in my life before.'

'Then who…?'

'My personal assistant. She came down, had a look to make sure that…'

'It wasn't going to be a dump?' Sophie filled in helpfully.

'Something like that.'

Sophie digested this. The man who had won her over with his humour and his intellect, who had shown himself to be surprisingly thoughtful, was little more than a rich snob. She vaguely recalled that that had been her initial opinion of him, which just went to show that first impressions were always the right ones.

'Because you couldn't possibly have stayed in a dump, could you? Maybe if you had really been a writer, even a well-to-do writer, you would have had some experience of financial hardship, but you never had that experience, did you, Theo?' How could she have missed it? The way he carried himself? That invisible mantel of authority that really only came to those accustomed to wearing it from birth? The cut of his clothes—even the clothes he used to hang around the cottage in? She had missed the obvious because, quite simply, she hadn't been looking.

'No. I have never had that experience. Look me up on the Internet if you want a potted history of my background. I live in London. I run my family's business as well as several of my own and I am worth a great deal of money. Gloria, my personal assistant, chose to tell the estate agent that I was a writer. Maybe she thought that there would be fewer questions asked about a writer taking time out here as opposed to a high level businessman. She may even have considered the possibility that someone around here might have heard of me.'

'And you never felt tempted to tell me the truth?' Sophie asked softly, lowering her eyes.

'What would have been the point? Would it have changed anything between us?' Theo raked his fingers through his hair. He felt like the worst possible heel. He could rustle up every argument in the book, could have told her that whether he had been a butcher, a baker or a candlestick maker, they would still have enjoyed their time together in the same way, but watching her face still made him feel ashamed of himself.

'No.' To Sophie's mind, he had probably told her everything she needed to know. 'No, I don't suppose it would have.' It changed *everything*. She had meant nothing to him after all. She hadn't been worth the effort of truthfulness. They had truly enjoyed a relationship that had been purely of the moment. No plans had ever been made to move forward and, as far as Theo was concerned, no mention had ever been made of the past.

'Why did you come here, Theo? Really? A cottage in Cornwall isn't the usual haunt of rich businessmen, even if the cottage is presentable enough.'

'Are you insulted that my personal assistant checked it out beforehand?'

'No,' Sophie said bluntly. 'And you haven't answered my question. Not, of course, that you have to.'

'Let's go into the sitting room, Sophie. It's uncomfortable having this conversation here.'

Sophie wasn't sure how much more of the conversation she needed or could even endure, for that matter. Her heart felt like lead. She shrugged and walked towards the sitting room. She seemed to be mocked at every step by reminders of the delusions of love she had stupidly nurtured. He had touched her right there, by the fireplace. Had pulled her down on to him on the sofa. Together they had stood by the window and looked out at the glorious scenery, their arms casually around one another. And, out of those little intimacies, she had concocted a dream of neverending happiness.

'My foot.' He sat down on one of the chairs, noting that she took the chair furthest from his. If Yvonne had been standing in the room, there was a very great possibility that he might have strangled her. 'I was told by my consultant that I needed to rest my foot or risk losing the use of it permanently. Since there was not a chance in hell that I could rest in London, I decided to take time out somewhere a reasonable distance away from my offices.'

'And she was…someone you left behind in London? Someone you were involved with? Or *are* involved with?' Sophie was proud of the measured control in her voice. No one would think that her heart was being ripped to shreds.

'She was never a *someone*,' Theo said grimly.

'You mean she was just a random stranger who got it into her head to drive down here and accost you?'

'No. I knew her, but not in the way you probably think.'

'In what way, then?'

'What's the point of all this cross-examining?' Theo rasped. 'Isn't it sufficient for me to say that I wasn't sexually involved with the woman—never had been and was never going to be?'

'No,' Sophie answered quietly. 'Not for me, at any rate. We

slept together and I think that gives me the right to have some of my questions answered. Naturally, if you don't want to do that, then just tell me…'

'What do you want to know?' There was a sickening air of inevitability about this. Theo consoled himself with the thought that their relationship had always had an inevitability about it. That, he told himself, had been part of its charm. The very temporary nature of its existence had added an urgent, hungry dimension to what they had enjoyed, and that could only have been a good thing. Surely.

'She said that you were *off women*…' Colour invaded her cheeks. However hard it was going to be, she had to have that question answered. 'I just wondered whether…'

'Whether…?' Theo could read the discomfort on her face and was at a loss as to what she wanted to ask him. Whatever it was, it could only add to the catastrophe of what had happened.

He frowned at the depth of emotion he felt, then he shook himself.

'Whether you're…confused…' Sophie said in a rush.

Theo was stunned into silence. 'Sorry. I don't follow you.'

'Yvonne mentioned that you were *off women*…'

'Yes, yes, yes. I got that part. It's the other part that I don't understand.'

'I wondered whether you had come here because you wanted time out to think about your sexuality…'

In the midst of the tension, which radiated around them in waves, Theo couldn't stop himself. He burst out laughing. He hooted with it until he had to hold his head in his hands. Eventually, the last remnants of his mirth died away and he looked at her seriously. As seriously as he could, at any rate.

'How, after all the times we've made love, could you have

entertained such a ridiculous idea?' he asked, only resisting the urge to laugh again because of the seriousness of her expression.

'Why else would you be off women?' Sophie asked defensively. 'Off them enough to come all the way down here? I wasn't to know that the reason had been your foot—I mean, I knew you had a bad foot, that you'd injured it, but I wasn't aware of the seriousness of it—but even if that was the real reason you came here, *what did she mean by that remark*?'

Theo looked at her steadily and knew, without a shadow of a doubt, that what he was about to say would end whatever they had for ever and leave it finished on a very bad note. This was definitely not the place he wanted to be when the time came for him to gather his belongings and leave Cornwall but he could see no way of evading the directness of her question. She would see right through that ploy, for a start. He realised, with sudden surprise and discomfort, that she seemed to know what he was thinking a lot of the time. She might not have had much of an inkling about his past, but she had damn well sewn up the present. When had he allowed that to happen?

He stood up and began prowling the room, restlessly aware of her eyes on him. Eventually, he went to the window and perched on the broad ledge.

'There's something I haven't told you. It's no secret but I didn't see the need to…trouble what we had by dragging bits and pieces of my history into it.'

You knew all the bits and pieces of my history, Sophie thought, but then again the choice to confide in him had been her own. More fool her.

'Oh, yes. And what would that be?'

'I was engaged. Once.' At a loss as to where to begin his explanation, Theo scythed aside the dross and went for the absolute fundamental. 'To a girl called Elena.'

'Oh.' Those skeleton facts were like a blow to Sophie's stomach. He had never once mentioned any significant other, had never hinted that he had had any kind of romantic past at all. She had credited him with women but never with a fiancée. He had never *lied* to her about his past; he had simply failed to mention the most important bits of it.

'Would anything have been gained by mentioning her?' Theo demanded aggressively, hugely, irritatingly rattled by the expression on her face. 'What would you have done? Sympathised? Held my hand? The past was well left where it was.'

Sophie stared at him for a few short seconds, hurt beyond words, then she looked down at her hands, making a conscious effort to keep them still.

He wasn't to blame. She knew that. He had never suggested that they had anything more than a casual sexual relationship. He had not seen the importance of sharing because sharing was something that constituted one of the building blocks of a proper relationship and the only one who had wanted a proper relationship in the end had been her. He had already had his proper relationship and it hadn't worked out.

'I suppose,' she mumbled. She took a deep breath and ventured a bright, ghastly smile. 'What happened? Or would you rather not tell me?'

The night before, when Theo had delivered Yvonne to the bed and breakfast and arranged her transport back to London, he had been subjected to hysterics. Tears and accusations. Female behaviour. Whenever he had broken up with a woman in the past, he had dealt with similar reactions. It was a familiar route. Sophie was not obeying the laws of expected female behaviour. She was clearly upset, but there were no tears or recriminations and he found that was much harder to deal with. Big mistake to have become involved with her.

CATHY WILLIAMS

149

'What do you want to know?' He made a conscious effort to distance himself mentally from her, but her face was tearing him up and he turned away abruptly to stare out of the window. It would be easier to talk to the gusty blackness outside.

'Well, what happened?'

'She died. An accident. There was nothing the doctors could do for her.'

'I'm so sorry, Theo.'

He glanced briefly at her. Her eyes looked huge in her pale face and he clenched his fists before returning to his chair so that he could put himself through the necessary torture of looking at her.

'When...when did this happen?'

'Twenty months ago.'

'Oh.' Like a jigsaw puzzle, Sophie was fitting the pieces together in her head and it was all making nightmarish sense.

Twenty months ago, Theo had been a happy man. Not the cynical one she had met, but probably a normal, relaxed, man, engaged to be married to a woman he loved. She didn't want to ask about Elena, but Sophie had no doubt that she would have been the perfect wife material. A man like Theo would never have settled for less. And then his dream had been shattered. She didn't need confirmation from him to know that the skiing accident involving his foot had been a result of grief and his efforts to expunge it. He was a hugely physical man. It made sense that he would have used the most physical outlet he could find for his emotions.

And he had gone off women. Most men might have been tempted to fling themselves into a series of affairs, but then Theo was not most men.

'Which brings me to what Yvonne said,' Theo told her. She

was wearing a faraway look on her face. Trying to work him out, he assumed, and probably arriving at all the right conclusions. Well, she was no fool and she knew him better than he would have liked. 'I haven't been involved with a woman since Elena's death.'

'But you've had no shortage of offers,' Sophie said slowly. 'And Yvonne must have just been a particularly persistent one.'

He didn't answer because there was no need.

'Poor woman,' she said, almost to herself, and Theo frowned impatiently.

'Why *poor woman*? Believe me, I never gave her any encouragement. I buried myself in my work and if women saw me as a challenge, then that was entirely their affair.'

Sophie stood up and walked across to the fireplace. It had suddenly become cold in the room and she busied herself lighting the fire. It was an open fireplace, and once upon a time there had been roaring fires there in winter, but five years ago they had installed a gas fire for the sake of convenience. Now, she wished she could lose herself in the mindless task of stoking a real one, buy herself time in which to come to terms with the painful ebb and flow of Theo's revelations.

Eventually, she straightened up and turned to face him.

'You'd been celibate for eighteen months?'

'Until I came here.'

Sophie would dearly have loved to have found some consolation in that fact, but in her heart she knew that there would be none. He didn't care about her—at least not in the enduring way she wanted—but she had to know why he had become involved with her in the first place. She wanted the full story before she walked out of the cottage.

She nodded and folded her arms tightly across her chest. 'Why me?' she asked calmly.

'I don't think it's a good idea for us to progress with this conversation,' Theo said flatly. 'I've given you what you wanted to know and, yes, maybe I should have told you before, even though there was no necessity…'

'I want to know why you decided to break your self-imposed celibacy and sleep with me. And don't tell me that it was because of my abundant physical charms. I've seen Yvonne. I know what physical charms you could have had in London and I don't compare.'

Theo felt a sudden overwhelming flare of anger at her ease in putting herself down. Without any trace of vanity, he knew that he could have had pretty much his pick of women. Before Elena's appearance in his life, he had slept with some of the world's most beautiful women and he could have told Sophie, without lying, that none compared to her. But, and this was where it got confusing, was that because a starving man would enjoy any meal presented to him? Had Sophie simply been the right woman in the right place at the right time? Hence the way she fulfilled him like no other? He decided that the theory ticked all the boxes.

'Well?' Sophie prompted. 'I've pretty much got the picture. I just need to have the gaps filled in.'

'Because it'll make you feel better?'

Sophie thought that there was nothing that could ever make her feel better. He would leave behind him a cold void in her life which would never be filled, but unanswered questions would make that coldness even worse.

'Because there's no point in telling half a story.'

'I slept with you because…' Theo felt his face darkening. It was one thing to be logical in his head, to tell himself that he had done absolutely nothing wrong. It was another matter to voice his thoughts to a woman who was looking at him as if she were seeing him for the first time and not really liking what she was seeing.

'Because you just couldn't resist me? My sparkling personality? Maybe you just found me challenging because I didn't make an effort with you, because you knew that I didn't want you in my cottage. Was that it?' Sophie took a few deep breaths and steadied herself because there was nothing to be gained from shouting, even if she really, really wanted to yell her head off. She had seen Yvonne and felt sorry for her because her emotions had been so plain to see and she wasn't going to leave Theo feeling sorry for her. Lord knew, he probably already did, but she wasn't going to compound the situation by shedding all her self-control.

'Dammit, Sophie! I slept with you because…*it felt right*!' And this, he thought, felt *wrong*, this cruel unravelling of what they had enjoyed.

'Why?'

'Because…' Theo glared at her and raked his hand through his hair. Then, as if he couldn't bear to sit still any longer, he stood up and began prowling through the room, avoiding her, pausing only when he spoke and only then looking at her ghostly pale face. 'Because…I was not in London, not surrounded by well-meaning friends and women who were rubbing their hands together at the thought of netting me. I even had a different identity here! A different occupation! I was no longer Theo Andreou, multi-millionaire carrying the burden of a dead fiancée. I was Theo, a writer, enjoying the peace of the Cornwall coastline and, yes, you came along and I wanted you.'

'I was your therapy,' Sophie said in a hollow voice.

'That is an ugly thing to say.'

'Ugly but true. People behave differently when they're removed from their normal surroundings. Did you know that? That's why, when people go abroad on holiday, they can become involved in all sorts of romances and truly believe that it's the real thing when, of course, it isn't. We did some psychology as part of our course and I remember thinking how true that was.' They were staring at each other, their eyes clashing. 'You came here and found that you could break the cycle and I was the one you broke it with.'

Theo turned away, his mouth set in a grim line, every muscle in his body rigid with distaste for the conversation he was having. But she was right. Being here had freed him from the tyranny of his grief, had allowed him to rediscover the pleasures of being a man, a red-blooded, sexual male. 'Which isn't to say that we didn't enjoy what we had.'

'No.'

'But it was never going to go anywhere. We both knew that. I never promised you anything but the moment.' He felt a dull ache inside him and propped himself up against the wall with the flat of one hand. He wanted to tell her that they could go on, could enjoy the remainder of his stay in Cornwall, pretend that Yvonne had never appeared, that the house of cards was still intact, but of course he knew what her answer would have been.

'No. No, you didn't, Theo.' Sophie looked down at the ground because it hurt too much to keep looking at him. 'I'm going to go now.' She willed her legs to move and they did. She pointed them in the direction of the door, which would have meant her brushing past him, and they obeyed. She even willed her body not to react to his proximity and no one, she hoped, would guess that she was a trembling, uncontrolled mess inside.

'Sophie…' Her name was dragged out of him and he closed his mouth before he could say something he shouldn't. Beg her to stay.

'I know,' she said over her shoulder. 'This was inevitable anyway. And don't worry; I don't blame you for anything.' She was putting on her coat now and moving towards the front door. 'I never expected anything.' That hurt but her hand was already on the door knob. Just one final look at the man she had fallen in love with. He was lounging against the banister, looking at her, hands shoved into his pockets. 'It just would have been nice…for you to have been a bit more open with me.' She let herself out quickly, before her self-control dissolved completely, and she literally ran the way back to her flat, head down against the blustery, snow-filled wind. She wasn't even aware of the bad weather. She was just aware of the massive effort it was costing her to hold back the tears until she reached the privacy of her own four walls and the thunderous, painful sound of her fanciful delusions crashing to the ground.

CHAPTER NINE

SOPHIE, facing the choice of going to London by car or by train, had chosen the train because she wanted, no, *needed* a relaxed journey, time during which she could marshall her thoughts and rehearse how she was going to handle the situation that had landed on her lap the previous morning.

Big mistake. The trip had been horrendous. Wet weather, unseasonably wet for March, or so someone had informed them all over a Tannoy system, had wreaked havoc with the tracks, causing delays on pretty much every line. There had been much hanging around stations, waiting for connections that failed to materialise on time and then, once on the train, overcrowding had left her spending fifty per cent of the trip on her feet.

She had thus arrived in London much later than expected and resembling something dragged backwards through a hedge.

Which, in turn, had necessitated a dash to the shops so that she could replace her jumper with something less sodden and purchase a pair of flats to take the place of her pumps, which had given her blisters.

And of course she could hardly walk into the building looking like a drowned rat and toting carrier bags bulging with wet, worn clothing. Not to mention the fact that it was too late to think about returning to Cornwall.

She booked herself into a cheap hotel in Earl's Court, dumped the bags there, did something with her hair and make-up and then looked at herself critically in the mirror.

It had been over three months since she had seen him. When he looked at her, she wanted him to see a woman in control of her life, a woman who neither needed nor wanted charity, a woman who had moved on.

Of course, she wasn't quite that woman, but just as long as he didn't spot that, then she was fine.

Sophie closed her eyes and breathed in deeply. She didn't want to be here, to be facing the man who still haunted her every waking moment and most of her sleeping ones as well. Least of all did she want to be striding into his office when everyone would be on their way out, leaving her alone with him. But that letter was burning a hole in her bag and she just couldn't face another sleepless night rehearsing what she was going to say to him, how she was going to feel.

So, although it was now after five, she would get to that office if it killed her.

At least she knew that he was going to be in. It had taken a bit of cunning but she had telephoned his personal assistant, asking for Gloria *by name*, introducing herself as an old friend of Theo's. The fact that she had been able to provide so many personal details of his life had worked in her favour. She wanted to surprise him, she had said to Gloria, with a woman to woman chuckle down the line. She knew that he didn't like surprises but they hadn't seen one another for a while and as she was in the country it seemed a shame to pass up the opportunity…

There was no way that she would travel up to London on

the off chance. Not when she knew, from the time she had spent with him, just how much he was out of the country. Research for his writing, he had always allowed her to assume. Making vast sums of money, she later discovered.

The person staring back at her convinced her that, image-wise at least, she was doing all right.

She looked smart in her grey skirt, white shirt with a darker grey V-necked jumper over it and black flats. Her hair, three months longer, was pulled back into a ponytail and she was only wearing a dash of lipstick.

She made sure to get a taxi to his office. Having rectified the damage caused after hours on public transport and by the vagaries of the bad weather, she wasn't going to risk arriving at his place of work drenched, sodden and exhausted.

It was after six by the time the taxi had manoeuvred through the packed London streets. The rain had slowed everything down to a virtual standstill. Sitting impatiently in the back seat, Sophie had to content herself with drumming her fingers on the car seat and repeatedly looking at her watch, agonisingly aware that the faster time ticked by the higher the chance that his office would be cleared of people, that she would be facing him without the comfort of other people around.

She wasn't sure what she was expecting, but when, at six-thirty, the taxi slowed in front of a forbidding glass house, she realised that the building she was staring at ranked pretty high on her list of what she really didn't want to find.

It was a few storeys high, smoked glass, and did not look welcoming. Sophie couldn't imagine anyone applying for a job there and actually walking through those doors to see what was inside. Surely fifty per cent would turn tail and run.

It was definitely what she felt like doing right now, but she paid the driver and strode towards the building, which, once inside, she found comfortingly alive with people and quite tastefully done with marble flooring and oversized plants in strategic places. A doughnut-shaped desk dominated the central space and behind it were three women who looked as though they had recently stepped off a catwalk. Sophie knew just what to say. She walked up to the least daunting of them and smiled. 'Gloria's expecting me,' she said. 'Floor three? I'm a bit late. I should have been here an hour and a half ago, but...'

'Are you the girl from Cornwall? I go there with my family on holiday every year. We stay at the Walker apartments. Gloria said that I was to send you up.'

On closer inspection, the catwalk model didn't look a day over eighteen and when she referred to her *family*, was doubtless referring to her mum and dad. Sophie relaxed just a little bit.

She hadn't expected to find the place quite so busy, but then you didn't make money by slouching and Theo Andreou made a lot of money. She had looked him up on the Internet and filled in all the blanks. His actual income wasn't listed, but, reading between the lines, she worked out that that would have been an impossible feat. There was too much of it, tied up in numerous companies and holdings.

The complex, thoughtful, arrogant, funny writer had turned out to be a legend in the world of finance and business.

She tried to remind herself that this was the truth of the matter, that she was going to confront a man who was a complete stranger and, even though they had slept together, she had never known him at all. So nostalgia would be a wasted emotion.

The third floor was as busy as it had been in the sprawling foyer. Sophie emerged from the lift to find it buzzing, even though it was clear that some of the workforce had already departed.

It was mostly open-plan but cleverly spaced out so that no one seemed to be intruding on anyone else. Plants were dotted around and the furnishings, blending in with the high-tech look of everything else she had seen so far, were chrome and cherry wood.

Sophie glanced around her, wondering in which direction Gloria's office was, and was rescued by Gloria herself, who approached her with a smile.

'The surprise visitor,' she said, standing back and taking a good look, while introducing herself.

'I'm so glad you're still here. I thought you might have gone home, but I honestly couldn't help being late. Dreadful delays on the trains and then the rain...'

They were walking away from the wildly plush working area towards a small foyer, complete with its own reception area, and as they walked Gloria explained the dynamics of a company where, seemingly, the employees were so motivated by responsibility and financial rewards that they never clock-watched.

Sophie looked around, reluctantly impressed by the surroundings. Little wonder he had been so casual in his spending. The sums of money that would sink most normal individuals, such as herself, would be insignificant drops in the ocean to him.

She resurfaced from her thoughts and realised that Gloria was now telling her that she hoped she, Sophie, would be able to get Theo out of his black mood.

Or add to it, Sophie thought, wondering, nervously now that she was finally here, how he was going to react to her. They had parted company on the very worst of terms. The good time girl he had wanted had turned into yet another female with demands and he probably breathed a hefty sigh of relief whenever she crossed his mind. If she did at all.

Alleviating whatever black mood dogged him was certainly not going to be something she would be able to achieve.

However, as a long lost friend, that was hardly the sort of confession Gloria would expect to hear, so, as they neared the imposing oak door, Sophie heard herself muttering something vague while her stomach did a few sickening flips and somersaults.

She steadied her fluttering nerves by placing a hand firmly on the clasp of her handbag, reminding herself why she was here in the first place.

'Have fun,' Gloria whispered and Sophie smiled weakly. 'I'll just tell him that he's got a visitor and the rest is up to you. He'll be so pleased to have news from home. I know his mother has phoned several times and she sounded quite worried, even though I assured her that his foot is back to new. You can get in touch with her and let her know how things are over here!'

Sophie nodded guiltily and wondered what had possessed her to embroider her story in such detail.

In the few seconds during which Gloria had disappeared into the office and then, judging from the opening of a further door, into an inner sanctum, Sophie indulged in a whirlpool of murky emotions, from anger through to guilt through to sheer terror.

But her expression was calm and controlled when she was ushered and left at the door to that inner sanctum, in which Theo sat behind a massive desk, absent-mindedly looking down and frowning at a report in front of him.

It only took a couple of seconds for Sophie to recognise a few crucial things. One was that he hadn't changed at all—

her memory had been picture perfect. The second was that she responded to him all the same crazy ways now as she had when she had last seen him three months previously.

She coughed to get his attention and, as he slowly looked up, she could feel herself falling, mesmerised, under the spell of his powerful masculine charisma.

For the briefest of time neither of them spoke. Sophie didn't think she could have, even if she had wanted to. Really, she could have just stood there and carried on falling into the depths of his shuttered green eyes.

Theo spared her the temptation by finally breaking the silence. 'Well, well, well. What a surprise.' He pushed himself away from the desk so that he was lounging back in his chair, looking at her. 'What can I do for you?'

'You know what you can do for me.' Released from the suffocating stranglehold of his stare, Sophie at last discovered her vocal cords and also the anger that had propelled her to make the journey as soon as she had found out what he had done. She walked towards him and stood right in front of his desk. It took every ounce of focused will-power not to be overwhelmed by memories of the times they had shared.

She remembered some wise piece of advice about the power of the present being the only thing that mattered, about the past and the future being utterly powerless in comparison.

'You can tell me what *this* is all about!' She rifled through her bag and whipped out an envelope, which she pushed towards him, then she straightened up and folded her arms.

Theo didn't rush to take the envelope. Instead, he relaxed back in his leather chair, hands clasped behind his head, and looked at her.

For the first time in three months he had a moment of stunning revelation. He had missed her. It made absolutely no sense. She had been a holiday romance, something enjoyable that had come along just when he'd needed it most, but investing it with properties beyond that would have been stupid.

Which, he thought, as his heart skipped a beat, didn't take away from the fact that he had missed her.

'Aren't you going to look at it?' Sophie threw at him.

'I know what it is so there's no need for me to look.' His green eyes tangled with hers and for a few seconds the feeling of suffocation was so strong that he had to loosen his tie. 'And this is neither the time nor the place for us to be having this conversation.'

'Really? And what is the right time and place, Theo?'

'Not the end of the evening in my office!' He stood up so abruptly that it took her by surprise and she stepped back, her eyes widening as her illusory sense of power as she towered over him, for the first time ever, was lost. He had whipped round his desk before she could retreat further and clasped his hand on her arm.

'I will not have you creating a scene here! Why did you not call me on my mobile?'

'Because…'

'You thought I might hang up on you?' The smell of her was overpowering his control. Just being this close to her, feeling the softness of her flesh under his fingers, was going to his head like incense.

'I wanted to see you face to face…!'

'Because you missed me?' he murmured in a savage undertone that sent a thrill of electric excitement rushing through her body.

She opened her mouth to deny any such thing. Her head had filled with anger at herself for responding to him and anger at him for daring—*daring*—to think that she was so pathetic that she had spent the past few months pining in his absence.

Theo hungrily watched her lips as they parted. He could feel her shaking under him and he suspected that it wasn't from desire, but dammit, he couldn't help himself. The catastrophe that had been his coping mechanism was swept aside beneath a tidal wave of longing and he bent into her, his mouth covering hers, kissing her like a dying man starved of water. He felt her soften, heard her gasp, and then she was pushing him away.

Theo immediately stepped back, but not far enough or quickly enough to avoid the stinging of her hand on his cheek as she furiously slapped him on the face. Slapped him! He didn't think that he had ever been slapped by a woman before and he reacted with instinctive speed, capturing both her hands in his and leaning towards her.

'Don't you dare raise your hand to me again, woman!' *This*, he thought furiously, was one *very* good reason why he was well off without her! What sort of woman raised her hand to a man?

'Then don't try kissing me again!'

'I don't know what possessed me to give you that money!' Theo growled.

'Snap! Because I don't know either!'

There was a knock on his door and Theo harshly told whoever the hapless soul was to clear off. 'We're going to continue this somewhere else,' he said grimly.

'Where?' Sophie rather liked his office for a showdown. With people milling around outside there was a limit to what could happen between them and, after that scorching kiss, she was reluctant to test her self-control further. She had only just managed to pull back and for a few seconds she had been totally lost. Her lips were still tingling from the feel of his mouth and her body was so sensitised that if he touched her again she felt as though she might just topple over the edge. 'I don't intend to stay long,' she carried on quickly, but he was already slinging on his jacket, much to her alarm. 'I just came to tell you that…'

'Not here!' Jacket on, he paused in front of her. 'And I don't want you acting like a fisherwoman when we walk through the office!'

Fisherwoman was so ridiculous an adjective for her that Sophie gasped before scowling at him.

'If I act like a *fisherwoman* around you, it's because you bring it out in me! Anyway, I was not *acting like a fisherwoman*!'

'A real lady doesn't hit a man, nor does she shout in public!'

'Oh, for goodness' sake! And a gentleman doesn't maul a lady or give her cause to shout!'

Theo was finding it hard to imagine why he had missed her but he knew that, for the first time in months, he felt invigorated. And in desperate, shameful need of touching her again.

He swept her out of his office, managing to stop and chat with a couple of his employees before he left, knowing that they would be burning with curiosity about the woman next to him. Then they were taking the lift down to the basement where he kept his car. In the centre of London secured parking was a prized commodity and often he left the car there when it was more convenient to grab a cab. Tonight he knew just where he was heading.

'Where are we going?' Sophie asked as they slowly drove out of the underground car park, up a ramp, towards an evening that was finally clearing of rain. 'Because if you think you're taking me back to your place, then you can forget it.' Memories of that kiss and the way her body had melted seared through her mind. He was, she thought, barking up the wrong tree if he imagined that he could sleep with her for old times' sake!

'What would you do if I did?' Theo asked silkily. 'It would certainly be a hell of a lot more private than going to a restaurant.'

Since privacy was the last thing Sophie wanted, she was quick to respond. 'I don't need *privacy* to have this conversation with you, Theo. And if you *were* thinking about heading towards your house or flat or whatever you have—mansion, probably—then you'd better have a rethink.'

'Or else…?'

'Or else I'll refuse to get out of the car and, furthermore, you'd be shocked exactly how efficient my lungs can be when it comes to shouting! And, in a busy place like London, I'd bet there'd be a crowd of people surrounding us if I did that within five minutes! Including someone with a camera…'

Theo was caught between frustration and wicked amusement. He hadn't grinned in weeks but he did now, just the merest shadow of one which she didn't notice as she was staring grimly in front of her.

'Good thing I was taking you to a wine bar I know where we can have privacy without you feeling threatened, then.' He made a sharp left, somehow finding short cuts that were relatively free of traffic, and ended up in a part of London she would never have recognised, only really knowing the more touristy parts.

'I don't feel *threatened* by you,' Sophie said feebly, letting herself out of the car and wondering why she had ever jumped to the conclusion that he had been taking her back to his place when that obviously had never been the case. If her heated imagination was playing tricks on her, then she would have to put a stop to it immediately.

'Maybe you feel threatened by yourself,' Theo mused, moving round to stand by her. He was feeling it again. That urge to touch her, to feel her soft body pressed against his. He'd never realised that the simple touch of a woman could hold him in thrall like this.

He realised that this was what he had been missing—physical contact with her. Theo's logical brain worked through the permutations of this realisation and came to the obvious conclusion. There was unfinished business between them. Yvonne had come along and ruined the remainder of their fling. Now destiny had brought her back and the problem could be rectified. He would get her into bed and ease the curious torment he had been going through for the past couple of months. And, whatever her protests, he knew, with that unerring instinct of his, that she still wanted him.

Sophie, aware of him next to her, waiting for her to take the bait, ignored his remark. She might have been soft in the head once but she wasn't going to go down that foolish road again.

She preceded him into the wine bar, which was half empty so early in the evening, and after scanning the area, headed for a table that was private without being too secluded.

She refused wine and opted for orange juice and, as soon as the drinks were in front of them, she took a deep breath and asked him why. Why had he bailed her out of her financial problems? How had he known how much money to give her bank manager? Had he thought that she would never find out about it?

Theo answered the last question first. No, he told her truthfully, he hadn't considered the possibility of her finding out.

'As for how much money I instructed my bank to transfer money to yours... Don't forget I was compiling that program for you. I had a fair idea from that what sort of debts you were facing. Not a huge amount in the great scheme of things.'

'Well, a huge amount for *me*,' Sophie told him quietly, 'and, in the great scheme of things, not an amount I would want to accept from you.'

'Why?' Theo asked her bluntly. 'We...we shared something...and you helped me, probably more than you know...'

'For which I'm due a financial reward?'

Theo flushed darkly, aware that for once his fine grasp of the subtleties of the English language had badly let him down. 'You're being ridiculous! That isn't what I am saying!'

'As good as,' Sophie responded hotly. 'It's how it sounds to me, at any rate!'

'In which case,' he said heavily, 'I sincerely apologise. I thought I might help you out, save you the nightmare of trying to make ends meet.' He thought of the times when they had lain in bed together, talking about some nonsense or other, and felt a pang of longing that hurt him like a physical ache. It was an ache that could be reached and cured by tying up the loose ends, by letting their fling take its course and wither away, which was what would have happened had circumstances not interrupted the smooth course of things. He looked at her and gave her a slow rueful smile.

'It wasn't meant as an insult and I am very...hurt that you would have seen it like that.' He waited for her to soften but she was still frowning and he almost clicked his tongue in exasperation. She could be as stubborn as a mule and the trait, he realised, had not diminished over the months.

'The money was not very much...' As soon as he uttered the words, Theo realised that he had made a grave tactical error. He could see it in the way she stiffened, her eyes flashing in immediate response.

'No. No, it wouldn't be to you, Theo. I do realise that. After all, you're worth…millions? Or don't you even know?'

'It's irrelevant how much money I have or don't have.'

'Is it? You saw me as a charity case and everyone knows that wealthy people love giving money to charity. It eases their consciences when they head off to the nearest car showroom to purchase the latest sports model to add to their collection!' Okay. So she was being unfair. But Sophie was finding it difficult to think straight. She was too aware of his green shuttered eyes on her face, too sensitive to the stirrings inside her and the memories that were playing tricks with her mind. She looked at him and wanted him and hated herself for it. Hated herself for wanting to reach out and remind her fevered body of what it felt like to touch him.

'You're being ridiculous.' He wanted to tell her that he couldn't think of anyone who would be insulted if he gave them money to help them out but he knew that he should probably keep that incendiary piece of wisdom to himself.

'How did you find out, anyway?'

'I went to see my bank manager about paying off the last of the mortgage on the cottage with some of the *windfall money* from those *mysterious shares* he had discovered *tucked away* in one of my father's files. He fetched out a file and then had to go and sort something out with a customer who was acting up with one of the cashiers and, while he was gone, I just happened to swivel the file towards me and there it was. Your letter.'

'If I hadn't come along, would you have taken the money from your ex? Even though you didn't feel a damn thing for him? Hadn't even slept with him? Just because he offered to marry you? Would you have accepted the money if there was a wedding ring attached to the end of it?'

'I…*that's not the point*!'

'It's only not the point because you don't want to discuss it from that angle. You might say that I saved you from the fate of having to tie yourself down to a man you didn't give two hoots about just because he was decent enough to bail you out with his savings. Maybe it's the savings part that you found more appealing. Maybe the fact that I have a lot of money makes you feel like a charity case. Would it have helped if I had been a poor, struggling…let's say…*writer*?' Theo shook his head in frustration and shot her a thunderous look. 'I don't want to be having this argument with you.'

'I'm sure you don't. I'm sure you really would rather not be seeing me at all…' The thought that rankled at the back of her mind, the one that nagged away at her morning, noon and night. The thought that he had found it easy to just walk away without looking back. She heard the wistful sadness in her voice with dismay and hurriedly continued, without pausing for breath, 'But, whatever your intentions were in giving me that money, you must know that there's no way I can accept it. That's why I've come. To work out some kind of arrangement whereby I can pay you back all of it.'

'You. Want. To. Pay. Me. Back. The. Money.'

'Yes. All of it. I can't accept it.'

'Why not?'

'Because…because it wouldn't be right. Not for me. Maybe for somebody else.'

Everybody else, Theo muttered under his breath. The waitress brought him over another glass of wine and he resisted the temptation to down the lot in one go.

'Okay. You can pay me back whenever you want. There's no rush.'

'I don't like debts. I'd give you it all back right now, but most of it's gone, as you probably expected. Paying off creditors. I have a little bit left over…'

'Keep it. Do what you want with it. Give it to your favourite charity.' He took a long mouthful of wine and then nursed the glass broodingly, waiting for her to speak, wondering how he could feel so damn alive in the company of a woman who was driving him crazy.

'We need to work out terms for the repayment. I've done a bit of jotting down.' Sophie rummaged in her bag and brought out a sheet of paper, the worse for wear, having been buried beneath the paraphernalia she kept in her handbag.

Theo glanced at the piece of paper thrust on the table in front of him and nearly smiled. He had used to tease her about her appalling lack of mathematical know-how. She'd never questioned how exactly he knew so much about finance and figures and would cheerfully accept every recommendation he put forward in connection with her progressively deteriorating accounts.

'I told you. I'm not interested in having any of the money back. I wanted to help you out and, if you can't accept my help in the spirit in which it was intended, then you can give the money away.' He shoved the piece of paper back at her.

'Well, I shall send the money to you and you can do what you want with it.' She stuffed the paper back into her bag. 'Well…' She cleared her throat. 'That's all I came to say.'

'How *are* you? You never said…' Theo leaned towards her. He reached out and captured her fluttering hand in his and linked his fingers through hers, brushing her thumb with his.

That casual touch had the effect of a match thrown on to

dry tinder. Sophie felt a rush of scorching heat race through her body. She knew she had turned bright red. She could feel her face burning.

'What do you think you're doing?' The protest should have been accompanied by a pulling away of her hand. Instead her hand stayed where it was and the protest was more of a cracked, feeble question.

'What do you think? I'm holding your hand, Sophie.' Theo sighed and tilted her chin so that she was forced to look at him. 'It feels good. Does it feel good to you too?'

Sophie didn't trust herself to answer.

'We weren't ready to come to an end,' he murmured, meaning it from the bottom of his heart. How else to account for the fact that since returning to London he had been unable to summon up any interest in the opposite sex, even though he had successfully managed to relegate Elena to his past? He raised her hand to his mouth and brushed his mouth along her knuckles, not taking his eyes from her still, stricken face.

He could kick himself for having brought her to a wine bar. He should have obeyed his dominant masculine instinct and just driven her to his apartment. No sooner had this thought entered his head than he wryly dismissed it. Sophie was just too feisty to fall in line with anyone's dominant masculine instinct.

But still. He regretted where they were—in a goldfish bowl where he couldn't really even stretch over to kiss her, although he *could feel* her softly wanting to yield to him.

'We still want each other,' he continued softly. 'I've thought about you and, now that you're here, sitting in front of me, I realise why…because what we had should not have ended when it did… When I kissed you in my office, Sophie, I could feel you kissing me back and your body was agreeing with everything I'm saying now…'

The look in his eyes was so urgent, so utterly compelling, that Sophie felt herself shudder, weakly aware of the quicksand gently drawing her under.

She gently wriggled her fingers free. 'No.' At the same time she reached down for her handbag, which she proceeded to place in front of her on the table, a physical barrier between them. 'We had our time. I didn't come to London to try and reconnect with you on any level, Theo. I came because I needed to sort out this business with the money.' How easy it would have been to snatch at that carrot he was dangling in front of her, when every bit of her wanted him. In her case, though, a little was a lot worse than none at all. 'You have your life here…' *as you made all too obvious* '…and I have my life elsewhere…'

She stood up, desperate to go while she was still ahead in the courage stakes. Theo could so easily cut the ground from under her feet and she had to get away before he did.

'I'll send my cheques to your office address,' she muttered, 'and, as I said, you can do what you want with them…'

And then she was gone. Out into the cool, dark, post-rain night, not looking back once. Something she was very proud of, at least for the moment.

CHAPTER TEN

IT TOOK Theo ten minutes to sit there at the table, first bewildered by the way his plan to seduce her all over again had gone down the tube. Then angry at the rejection. How dared she *trick her way into his office*, his *sanctuary*, and create a scene over nothing? No, worse. Not over nothing. Over the fact that he had been *generous, thoughtful and bloody magnanimous* considering their relationship had come to an end! Not only had he *given* her the money to cover all her debts and then some, but he had done so *anonymously*! Was it his fault that she had chanced upon the letter because her bank manager happened to be indiscreet? No! And yet, for all his kindness, her response had been to fling it all back in his face!

Theo, paying the bill, was suddenly very much aware that his knowledge of the opposite sex was far more fragile than he'd thought.

Only after the anger had worked its way through his system did the full impact of her vanishing act hit him. Something else filtered its way into his head as well, and this made him sit back down heavily, frowning.

Then the certainty that he had to find her was like a sledgehammer blow.

Naturally, the night had swallowed her up. As luck would

have it, she had managed to find a taxi or else she had walked towards the nearest underground station, wherever that might be. Theo didn't know. He hadn't travelled on the tube for years.

Nor did he know where she would be staying that night, or even if she *would* be staying overnight in London. For all he knew, she was en route to catch the next available train back to Cornwall. Back to her ex. Because the nebulous thought that had been stirring at the back of his mind had found some fertile soil and taken root. How else was she going to manage to pay him back his money if not with the help of her very obliging ex-boyfriend?

Part of his decision to give Sophie that money had been a subconscious attempt to slice Robert out of her life completely. Financial independence would make his presence on the scene unnecessary. It was a very simple equation for Theo to grasp because, as far as he was concerned, Sophie felt nothing for the man but affection which seemed to have been based on a mixture of nostalgia and gratitude. Expendable emotion in the big scheme of things.

Now it occurred to him that his notion had backfired badly.

He, for reasons best known to herself, had assumed the role of big bad wolf, which made the ex—what? Knight in shining armour?

Theo wasted a few seconds deciding that he didn't care one way or another, that he had put her behind him once and he would obviously do so again. If she wanted to send his money back to him in some kind of churlish fit, then he would let her. There were charities that would benefit from her childish pique.

The confident mood swing didn't last long. He made a brave attempt to convince himself that the sudden bleak loss of self-control was due to the unexpected derailment of his plans. She had reappeared in his life out of the blue and he had realised that he still desired her, still wanted her in his bed. Instead of predictably allowing herself to be persuaded back in, she had walked out. That, he told himself, accounted for the sickening flood of panic washing through him.

He made just one phone call before speeding out of London.

If, on the other side of London, Sophie had not been indescribably tired, she would have made the trip back down to Cornwall that very night.

She just wanted to be back in the cottage and in her own bed. Enjoying both while she still could, because one thing was certain—finding the money to repay Theo would mean the inevitable sale of the cottage. She had managed to tie up all the loose ends, thanks to the money he had sent to her, via her lawyer. She now had a very clear picture of it all unravelling just as quickly.

And owing Theo…

How could she truly put him behind her if she still owed him a packet of money? Would she have to see him again? Talk to him on the telephone?

In a year's time, would she pick up her receiver to hear that dark, velvety voice of his? And what would it do to her mental health? Because seeing him again had been a nightmare. She had imagined herself to have built up some control but withstanding his impact had been like trying to withstand a gale balancing on one foot.

And when he had looked at her, kissed her…all the puny reassurances she had made to herself about being in charge of her emotions, all the self-righteous anger she had felt about the way he had walked out of her life without a backward glance, had vanished like a puff of smoke.

She had felt naked and defenceless and still hopelessly in love with him.

She couldn't understand how emotions could be so cruel. Why had it been so easy for her to turn away Robert—decent, kind Robert—in favour of someone who had twisted her up inside and spat her out? How could she still be so ridiculously in thrall to a man like that?

The next day Sophie travelled back down to Cornwall with fresh resolve. She would leave the sale of the cottage and the division of the proceeds to her lawyer. She trusted him and knew that he would deal with repaying Theo without hesitation. And she would leave the area. Not to go to London, because London would always be a cruel reminder of the man she had fallen in love with. No, she would go to stay with one of her university friends in York. She was sure that Ellie would put her up for free, at least temporarily, until she found her feet. In time she might resume her interrupted teacher training course, but until then she would get work where she could find it and at least have the blessed advantage of escaping all reminders of Theo. The reminders of her father she would always carry inside her. She didn't need the cottage as tangible proof that his presence was still with her.

In other words, she would be strong and proactive instead of pathetic and wistful.

The resolve lasted the duration of the train journey and it was, thankfully, a trip not plagued with poor weather and un-reasonable delays.

But then the darkness of the cottage when she finally got back was a stark reminder to her of the journey she had travelled in recent months. The trauma of her father's death, the stress of his undisclosed debts, and finally Theo, the brilliant light on her horizon that had turned into the blackness of a nightmare.

She let herself into the cottage quietly. Normally she would have gone straight to the kitchen, made herself a cup of tea, sat down and reflected on the day's events.

Tonight, however, she broke with routine and was heading towards the sitting room when a small noise alerted her to the presence of someone else in the house. Someone behind her. Sophie felt the hairs on the back of her neck bristle as footsteps neared and then, without pausing for thought, she did the first thing that instinct commanded. She swung around, bag first.

Sophie's bag, which held everything bar the kitchen sink, hit Theo across the face with such force that it drove him into a stumble and he impacted against the wall at the same time that Sophie switched on the overhead light, hand raised in case she needed to repeat the exercise.

Her eyes locked with Theo's and she gave a little squeak of shock.

'What are *you* doing here?' Her brain was frantically trying to work out the situation but the bizarreness of it was making her giddy.

'Being attacked with a great deal of ferocity,' Theo answered, rubbing the side of his face with one hand.

'I don't understand. What are you doing here? How did you get here? Before me? I left you...'

'Have you got a couple of paracetamol? I think my face might be reacting to the weight of your handbag.'

Quips about intruders deserving what they got flew out of her head as her eyes took in his face and the red bruise already beginning to rise up to the surface. Without saying a word, she dashed to the kitchen and returned with two tablets and a glass of water. He had already moved into the sitting room.

'I've been wondering how you intend to get your hands on that money if you want to pay me back,' Theo announced, swallowing the tablets and looking at her steadily.

'What?'

'The money. The ridiculous repayment idea you came up with…'

'It's not ridiculous!'

'Call me stupid, but it would prey on my mind if your need to pay me back ended up driving you straight into the arms of that ex of yours.'

'You came here to tell me *that*? How did you get here anyway?'

'Helicopter. How else? And yes, I flew here to tell you that.'

Sophie stood by the door and folded her arms. 'Okay. You won't be driving me into the arms of anybody. As a matter of fact, Robert has found someone, the daughter of one of his parents' friends. He met her when he went up to stay with them. Satisfied?'

Disproportionately so. 'Were you disappointed?'

Sophie clicked her tongue impatiently, wanting him out of her house but dreading his inevitable departure. She wondered whether this was some perverse ploy on his part to torture her because she had rejected his advances and then thought that he didn't care sufficiently for her to warrant such behaviour.

'If that's all you came to tell me, then you can leave now, Theo. I'm very tired. I just want to get to bed and go to sleep.'

'I'm not ready to leave.'

Sophie shook her head in disbelief and ventured a few incredulous steps into the sitting room, arms still folded. 'You're not ready to leave,' she repeated slowly, her mouth going dry as she stood in front of him, affected and hating it.

'I need to talk to you, Sophie…' Theo told her roughly, looking away.

'We've already talked.'

'Not…not about…money.'

'About what, then?'

He flushed darkly and glanced up at her tight expression. Hell, she was as unyielding as a rod of steel, but who could blame her? He had nonchalantly pretended to be someone he wasn't, had bedded her because—or so it had seemed to him at the time—it had seemed the right place and the right time, never mind her feelings, and, when held to account, had disappeared back to London without a backward glance.

Little wonder she had thrown back his gesture of money. That had probably been the last straw.

'I looked back,' he told her abruptly and Sophie frowned, bemused by the statement but reluctant to open up any conversational doors. The more she spoke to him, the weaker her resolve became. 'When I left the cottage. I looked back. Thought of you.'

So much so that you failed to pick up the phone and get in touch, Sophie thought, remembering how she had hoped with pathetic desperation for that phone to ring. She didn't say anything, just shrugged.

'I should have told you who I was,' Theo admitted. 'But it really didn't seem very important to begin with and after… Well, after…it would have been more difficult…'

'But not impossible. Look, I really don't see the point of discussing any of this. What happened, happened. I just want you to go now so that I can get on with my life.'

'Meaning that you can't get on with it while I'm around?'

'Meaning that I'm tired and I want to go to sleep. I didn't invite you down here. How did you get in, anyway?'

'Phoned our mutual friend, Mr Soames, your lawyer. He's a key holder for you. He let me in.'

'Money talks…' Sophie muttered, turning away, but,

before she could retreat, Theo's hand snapped out and he gripped her by the wrist, pulling her towards him so that she teetered and fell on to the sofa, on top of him.

Sophie writhed and wriggled in horror but was prevented from leaping to her feet by one very firm hand which was still circling her wrist.

'Please let me go,' she said very quietly, and Theo shook his head.

'I would if I could,' he muttered harshly. 'Do you imagine I want to have my entire life disrupted like this? Do you think I wouldn't rather find the determination from somewhere to carry on with my life?'

Sophie felt herself go very still. She risked a glance at his face but he wasn't looking at her. He was staring broodingly at the ground so there was no way that she could interpret his expression.

'I was a mess when I first came to Cornwall,' he said, still staring at the ground. Actually, talking to the ground rather than to her, so that she had to strain to hear what he was saying. 'I wouldn't have admitted that to anyone, but I was. I hadn't recovered from Elena's death. It was almost as though I had reached the next stage of my life—choosing the perfect woman to be the perfect wife to have the perfect kids—' he glanced up at her pale, impassive face and wanted to touch her so badly that it hurt '—and just when I thought it was within my reach, poof, it was gone.'

Sophie heard the words *perfect woman, perfect wife, perfect kids* and went cold inside. She hadn't known, but she'd been competing with a ghost. A *perfect* ghost. She had never stood a chance of winning the fight for Theo's heart. In fact, she wouldn't have come within five yards of him had it not been for the fact that she had been around at a time when he had been emotionally vulnerable.

She knew what it must be costing him to admit to vulnerability of any kind and she tried very hard to smile sympathetically, but her mouth just couldn't do it.

'The thing is…' Theo said softly, 'I never stopped to consider that there is no such thing as perfect, that I had put Elena on to an impossible pedestal and, before I could really discover the flesh and blood woman on top of the pedestal, she died, leaving me clutching a mirage.' He looked at her levelly. 'Then I came here, condemned to rest because of my foot, expecting to spend my time working on my laptop, communicating with the office and counting the days till I could get back to the real world. And I found you.'

'You should have told me that there had been someone else in your life…' *Someone you had loved,* she thought. Not that it would probably have made much difference. Her heart had taken off like a galloping horse and would have done whatever his story.

'Sometimes we hold things so close to our hearts that we forget the healing power of talking. The point is this, Sophie… You were real. Flesh and blood. You had a mind of your own and a tongue that wasn't afraid to be forthright. You were a living, breathing human being…'

'And, don't tell me, just what you needed to help you thaw out from the deep freeze you had put yourself into…I was useful…'

'You were useful…'

Sophie flushed, gutted by his easy agreement with her statement, yet there was no reason for him to lie.

'Or at least that's what I told myself. Would you look at me when I'm talking to you? I want to see the expression on your face because you have the most beautifully expressive face of anyone I've ever known.'

'If you cared that much about my beautifully expressive face, you would have…' Sophie stood up abruptly and walked towards the far window, where she stood looking at him, well away from his suffocating proximity.

'Stayed…? Asked you to leave with me…?'

Sophie remained resolutely silent, ashamed because those were the very things she had hoped for as the time had drawn near for his departure.

'Kept in touch,' she said, raising her head, daring him to challenge her. 'You had your demons, but I wasn't to know that. You walked away, Theo, and you didn't look back. If I hadn't chanced upon that letter of yours and decided to come up to London, you would have been quite happy to put all of this behind you as just another learning curve. Well, it's not good enough for you to come down here and try to clear your conscience by telling me that you thought about me, after all!'

'I've come down here to ask you to marry me.'

And he had. He hadn't realised it until now, but the words were out and he knew that it was absolutely what he wanted. Not for her to move in with him, not for the occasional weekend in Cornwall when he could find the time. He wanted her—all of her—all of the time. He wanted to climb into the same bed as her at night and awake to find her lying next to him.

'You must know I can't accept,' Sophie said quietly.

Theo, still smiling from the rosy picture in his head, frowned and tilted his head to one side, wondering whether he had heard properly. 'Sorry? You must have misheard me, Sophie. I just asked you to marry me.' He gave her a crooked smile and rose to his feet, covering the distance between them in a couple of easy strides. Because she hadn't moved and a chill of apprehension was beginning to infiltrate his pleasant mental scenario.

'How can I accept, Theo?' Sophie mumbled, stiffening as he folded his arms around her. Lord, but she had missed the warmth of his embraces, the unique woody smell of his aftershave, the feel of his hard body against hers.

'How can you not?' Theo said urgently, fighting down a weird clawing sense of panic.

She tried to push him away but he wasn't having any of it. He tightened his arms around her, willing some of his heat to melt the defences she had constructed around herself.

'I can't settle for being second best.' Sophie wondered why she was turning down the best thing to have ever happened to her. She clenched her fists against his chest to stop herself from giving in because living in the shadow of a ghost was not the basis for any kind of happy ever after fairy tale.

'What are you talking about, woman?' Theo tilted her face so that she was looking at him. In a minute she would burst into tears but, with that gritty inner strength of hers, she was holding on to her self-control. It was just one of the things he loved about her.

'I could never live up to the perfect fiancée who never made it up the aisle, Theo,' Sophie told him bluntly.

'You haven't listened to what I've just said…'

'Yes, I heard every word!'

'You're irresistible when you're wearing your stubborn hat…'

Sophie fought down the temptation to yield and glared at him mutinously. 'Don't try and soft soap me, Theo.'

'Then believe me when I tell you that you don't have to live up to anyone.' He paused, marshalling his thoughts and marvelling that it should have taken his long for him to face the truth. 'This is hard for me to say, Sophie, because I spent a long time clinging to the illusion that Elena was the only woman for me.' He stroked her hair as she continued to glare at him suspiciously. 'The truth of the matter is that I barely knew her. It wasn't just that I put her on a pedestal, as I said, but we spent relatively little time together. Looking back now, I don't honestly believe that it was a relationship that would have survived. On paper, she was the perfect woman. All the right connections and willing to serve her man. Truth is, you're the first woman I ever met who stood up to me and you're what I need…'

He tentatively kissed her on the mouth and was heartened when she didn't pull away. 'I know you care about me, Sophie. Marry me and I'll prove to you that I'm good husband material. You won't be walking in the shadow of a ghost. You're the only woman I have ever loved and the only one I ever will…'

'What did you say?'

'I love you.' Theo smiled slowly and kissed the tip of her nose. 'I would have come back, you know, if you hadn't shown up at my office yesterday. Life's been hell without you. So…will you marry me, Sophie?'

'I'm going to burst into tears any minute now,' she told him in an unsteady voice and he grinned at her.

'I know. So answer me quickly before you do…'

'Yes!'

'Then don't cry!' He kissed her on the mouth and, as she melted against him, he stroked her under her jumper, running exploring hands along her spine. 'I can think of other ways of celebrating our life together than shedding tears…'

Our life together? The most wonderful words Sophie had ever heard for a future that she had thought would never happen.